SPIRITUAL GUARDIANS OF THE ANDAMANS

BIPIN MENON

Made with ♥ on the Notion Press Platform
www.notionpress.com

Contents

CHAPTER I

Pearl Necklace

A paradise of islands adorning the sub-continent like a pearl necklace, the Andaman and Nicobar provide a bewitching sight that embellishes the Bay of Bengal. Land masses that are actually the tip of a submerged mountain range, they dot the vast expanse of the crystal clear blue waters with the multi-hued patches of green, brown and white.

As a quote goes, "*Andaman Islands is one such place that will revive your senses.*

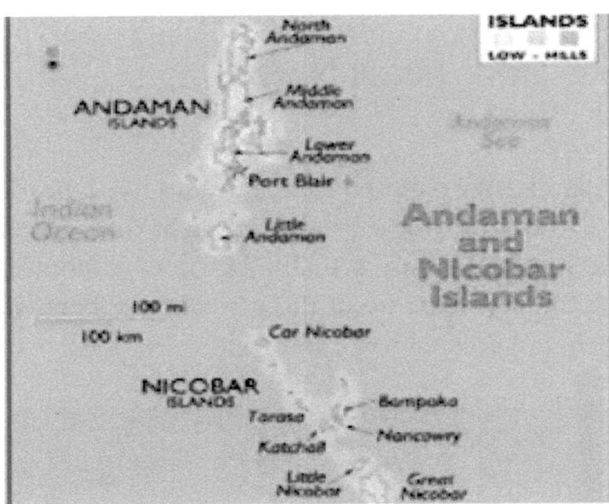

Both the island chains have their own uniqueness. They house islands of ancient mysteries, where time has etched stories into the sands and the rainforests.

The turquoise of the sea rivals the emerald of the jungle, a symphony of nature's finest hues. It has some of the most spectacular beaches in the world. The powdery white sands that attract tourists in hordes. The surface seems to provide a cushion effect and its almost akin to walking on a velvety carpet, welcoming all those who traverse it. Then there are the rocky beaches trapping within its crevices a wealth of flora and fauna. Crabs scurry in and out of their rock shelters while a variety of fishes dot the small waterpools that form amidst these rocks during the high tides.

The waters are some of the most transparent and clean. As one view the shores, the colours change from shades of white to turquoise to blue to green. It seems as if an artist has splashed colours and stroked the surface with his brush. It looks like an intermingling of different marine civilisations all separated by colour. Below the water surface is a wealth of marine life teeming with colour and activity.

The coral reefs dot the seafloor and shelter within it an array of fish species. They are among the most biodiverse marine ecosystems on the planet

The coral reefs house some of the most diverse species of marine life. There are fishes and crustaceans of all hue and colours, all giving a surreal feeling to the waters below. The shades of the coral reef add to the beauty of the eco-system. It is as if nature had etched a masterpiece by splashing colours into the blue turquoise waters. As someone said, "*There was no greater wonderland on Earth than the community of corals and fish. They sung of living in their colors, a sort of visual choir seen by the eyes and heard by the soul.*"

There are mangrove forests with canals traversing it. The roots of the plants that survive the ingress of salt water and provide stability to the vegetation.

The beds are full of the sashaying seagrass making it a feeding ground for dugongs and sea turtles. The mangroves are hotspots for crabs, fish and shrimps. The main source of food for these marine species is the plankton which is bioluminescent. The mangroves adapt to the tidal flow of water when it makes it ingress into the forests.

As Toni Morrison said, "*All water has a perfect memory and is forever trying to get back to where it was.*"

A number of marine species thrive in these clear waters. There are around nine different reefshark species including the large whalesharks.

Apart from this there are the Manta Rays which can grow upto three metres. Dugongs are herbivorous mammals which flourish in these waters. There are a number of species of turtles like the green, hawksbill and loggerhead. One can also see octopuses and cuttlefish in these waters. Then there are the moray eels which hide in crevices both as a defensive tactic as well as for making those surprise attacks.

It is indeed a paradise teeming with flora and fauna.

The rainforests are dense, virgin and lush green.

While much of this has been preserved in its pristine form, there are other parts which inhabited including by the indigenous people. Multilayered, they form a canopy from the harsh rays of the sun. There are both the evergreen and deciduous species of flora in the islands. There are ferns and orchids in the South Andaman islands. There are around two hundred different species of timber in the islands. Some of the common trees include the gurjan, sundari and coconut. As someone quoted, "*In the untouched forests of the Andaman Islands, every creature plays a role in the intricate web of life.*"

. The indigenous species of the Andaman islands include the serpent eagle, crake, hornbill, bulbul, drongo, shama, nightjar, scops owl, teal, sea eagle and doves.

The avian visitors which include egrets survive on fish and crustaceans. Kingfishers can be seen perched branches eyeing quietly the fish below. Stealth and silence are the name of the game The Nicobar islands have the endemic species like the pigeon, bulbul, sparrowhawk, sea eagle, doves, flycatcher and parakeet. The chirping and calls of these species brings forth vivacity in the dense undergrowth.

One of the most pervasive species is the wild pig which is found in nearly all the inhabited islands of the archipelago.

The long tailed macaque and the crab eating macaque are two of the species of monkeys which have adapted well to the eco-system of the islands. Barking deer was a species introduced to the island and has adapted well. The Nicobar flying fox is a fruit bat which plays a critical role in pollination by dispersal of fruits. The civet is one of the nocturnal predators in the forests that are bereft of the larger ones.

There is no doubt that these islands are a paradise for any visitor. In the words of Russel Banks, "*Each island is a world of its own, a singular, self-contained little universe.*" It charms them with its varied shades and beckons one to explore. It is nature in its rawest form nursing a wide spectrum of species. Despite all the specks of modernity, it retains it old world charm. The presence of the indigenous people co-habiting with the settlers is what makes it a unique human ecosystem. When Aristotle said, "*In all things of nature there is something of the marvellous*", he was probably referring to these islands.

CHAPTER II

Indigenous people and their history

In this archipelago, every island tells a story, each wave carries a memory. They stand as sentinels of a forgotten world, their shores whispering tales of resilience and survival. This resilience and survival instinct is specially manifested in the indigenous people who inhabit these islands. Historically, they are believed to have come from Africa and the South East Asia. Many of them still live the way of their ancestors with limited or no contact with outsiders. Despite the advent of colonial powers and the subsequent settlement from mainland India, some of them have managed to preserve much of their culture and tradition. The local administration has also managed to ensure the survival of these traditions without interfering with their way of life. However, some others have integrated with mainstream society and are playing an active role in its economic and social milieu.

The earliest reference to the islands and its people is in a work called Geographia, written around 150AD, by **Claudius Ptolemy** who was a Greek geographer. It mentions a number of islands where the people were naked and cannibals. The islands were also mentioned by **I-ching**, the Chinese origin buddhist monk of the 7th century, referring to it as the country of the naked people. **Abu Zaid Hasan** and **Sulaiman**, two Arab travellers during the 9th century also mentioned the islands referring it to as Najabalus. The islands were an important entrepot destination for the trade routes from China to the Arabian peninsula. The Venetian traveller **Marco Polo** gave an account of the islands in 1290 AD calling it Angamanian. But his account speaks of the inhabitants in a derogatory manner speaking of them having heads like dogs with canine like teeth and eyes. He further described them as a cruel race which feasted on outsiders. A Francisian Missionary, **Friar Odoric** during his voyage around 1332 AD while referring to cannibalism and dog faced features provided a perspective of their social practises where the traditional marriage practises did not exist and women were common. **Nicolo Conti**, an Italian traveller during 1440 AD called the island Andamania or the Island of Gold. His description provided a different perspective on the economy stating that the people wore earrings of gold, dressed in cotton and silk clothing, lived in low houses and practised idolatory. However, he did mention about the cannibalistic practises of the islanders. The Italian traveller **Cesare Frederici** who travelled to the islands in 1567AD mentioned the islanders as primitive and aggressive in intent. The fact is that the derogatory connotations come only from European travellers and would have to do with both their general attitude towards the Oriental civilisations and the islanders safeguarding their own survival. The legendary Maratha naval commander **Kanhoji Angre** is said to have used the islands around the late 17th century as a temporary base to thwart the European ships sailing to the East.

The aggressive behaviour especially of the Sentinelese is manifested by the attacks on ships which berthed or were shipwrecked. In 1844, there was on such attack on the shipwrecked crew. The British expedition in 1867 was attacked by the Onges. A number of incidents involving the Sentinelese have been documented. In the same year of the Onges attack, a ship Nineveh came ashore on the Sentinel and the crew were attacked with iron tipped spears. In 1981, a ship PMV Primrose was stranded in the sea and they launched an attack with 50 canoes. However, they were unable to board the ship due to the rough seas. Even as late as 2004, when a Coast Guard helicopter went for a post tsunami rescue mission to the North Sentinel, it was attacked with arrows, some of which went upto 100 feet and hit the chopper. Subsequently, in 2006 two fishermen were killed while in 2018 a missionary was killed in his attempt to proselytise the Sentinelese.

However, the larger picture has to be looked at. The indigenous people of the island have their own unique culture which is premised on sustainability with nature. Ironically, the ones who came into the mainstream society lost their cultural roots and have actually forgotten the life that their ancestors led. On the contrary, the ones who have been aggressive towards outsiders have been able to preserve their heritage. The entire series of incidents have to be looked upon in the light of a fight between the ancient roots and modernity.

The penal settlement of the colonial powers also had an adverse effect on the indigenous people. The first of these was established in 1789 in Port Cornwallis. Though it was abandoned in 1796, a new one came up in Port Blair in 1858 after the first war of independence. It also had the Wahabi fighters and the Burmese rebels. The notorious Cellular Jail came up in 1908 and this led to a wave of anti-colonial fighters being lodged. It was only the brief Japanese rule in 1942 that saw the start of the end of this penal colony.

The colonial rule also did a lot of damage to the indigenous people. The British rule saw a number of unsavoury incidents with the indigenous people including picking them up from their settlements and taking them to Port Blair. Firstly the attitude towards the indigenous population was far from conciliatory and there were many skirmishes that occurred. Retaliatory attacks were also carried out by the tribesmen. However, the more dangerous development was the spread of diseases contracted due to the clearance of forests and interaction with the inmates of the penal settlement. The lack of immunity lead to a large number of deaths. The Japanese rule was also pernicious for them as fighting with heavy armour around their habitation occurred. It displaced them as they were caught in the middle.

The Shompens

Shompen

The **Shompen** inhabit the island of Great Nicobar which is pristine and has a forest cover of around 95%. Those on the western side of the island are known as Kalay while the ones in the eastern part are Keyet. The refer to each other as Buavela. They are believed to be the ancestors of the Mesolithic hunter gatherers of the Southeast Asian region who came to the island around 10,000 years back. The proximity of the island to Indonesia gives credence to this theory since their features are also Mongoloid. The first contact with this tribe-was made in 1846 by Admiral Steen Bille, a Dutch explorer. Subsequently, the Danish turned British citizen Frederick Roepstorff collected the ethnographic and linguistic data on the tribe in 1876. They are considered a particularly vulnerable tribe with the population severely impacted during the Great Tsunami of 2004 with the numbers plummeting to around only 50. However, they are now believed to be around 200-300. As hunter gatherers, they are dependent on bows and arrows for hunting of animals like crocodiles, lizards, monkeys and wild boar. They scurry the forests for gathering edible fruits like pandanus and honey. They also practise shifting cultivation by growing root vegetables, yam and tobacco. The are semi-nomadic in nature, firstly by establish temporary settlements of local material. Once the resources are exhausted, they move to other regions allowing for natural regeneration. The thatched huts are built on stilts to keep off the potential danger from the ground elements. The walls are of wood with woven material. The roofs are made of thatched palm fronds. There are sleeping mats on the floor. The utensils are hung on the wall or the rafters which support the roof. The attire is minimal with men wearing only a loincloth made of bark cloth. The women normally wear a knee length skirt with a shawl made of the same material. They also wear jewellery made up of bamboo such as beads, bands, necklaces and plugs. Living in such an environment, they have a sound knowledge of the ecosystem. This enables them to identify edible plants and understand animal behaviour which aids them in both gathering and hunting. However, the contact with outside world has increased and in the general elections, some of them even exercised their franchise.

The Jarawas

Jarawas

The **Jarawas** inhabit the dense vegetation of the Southern Andamans. Evidence suggests that they may have come around two millenium ago. Given their physiological features, it is believed that they came from the African continent or from parts of South Asia. As usual the colonial rule and settlements by outsiders had a debilitating effect on them due to the advent of infectious diseases. They were denizens of the lower parts of South Andamans but got displaced. However, they managed to occupy the western part of the island and even the Middle Andamans Island with time. It was the displacement of the Great Andamanese tribe which enabled them to occupy the swathe of land in the Middle Andamans Island. Today, this is one of the tribes that has the most frequent interaction with outsiders on account of the Grand Andaman Trunk road which passes through the dense forests. The interaction has led to a lot of exchange of goods, special hospitals and schools for the tribe. Some of them have managed to learn the language and a number of elders help in the conservation of the lands of these people. Some people remain skeptical of these interactions and with some unpleasant ones, the courts have put a lid on the passage of tourist vans through this road. Their number is around 300 and the tribe has managed to survive the passage of time. They primarily undertake hunting but also are adept at fishing. They forage for agricultural produce in the forests. They are armed with bows, arrows and spears and known to be fierce warriors defending their territory. The arrow heads are made of both iron as well as areca nut or bamboo. They also wear a chest guard known as kekad during these hunting expeditions There have been incidents of attacks on outsiders including workers building the trunk road. They hunt animals of the forests like wild pigs and monitors with bows and arrows. They have begun the use of dogs for hunting animals. Fishing is also a key economic activity with some of them using canoes to go to other islands to fish. They use bow and arrows as well as baskets to catch marine creatures in shallow waters. These include fish, molluscs, dugongs and turtles. Foraging in the forests is primarily carried out for fruits, tubers like yam and honey. The platter is broad and some of it is consumer raw. However, they are known to boil, roast or bake it too. The government has provided them support to grow citrus fruits plantations.

The Sentinelese

Sentinelese

The **Sentinelese** are the most protected of the tribes as they have scant history of interface with outsiders. They inhabit the North Sentinel Island, a very large expanse of around sixty square kilometres on the western side of the South Andaman island. There are various theories about their origin. The most common being that they came from the African continent. However, there is another school which says that they were originally from the Little Andamans but were caught in a cyclone while fishing in the sea. The canoe they were in drifted towards the North Sentinel. But the fact that the language is quite different from both the Jarawas and the Onges lends less credence to this theory. However, on the other cultural aspects, they seem very close to the indigenous people of the islands who are of Negrito stock. Physically, they are larger and better built than the Jarawas and Onges who are also believed to come from Africa. The food habits such as hunting, gathering, fishing and the semi-nomadic lifestyle. They roam the forests for fruits, wild honey, nuts and other edible produce. Agriculture, even the shifting one has not been observed. Hunting of animal is widely prevalent and is an important source of food though the tribesmen have been seen to eat raw meat. Pigs and turtles are the main source of sustenance for the tribe. However, when compared to the other indigenous people, they catch fish both in the shallow sea as well as in the deeper waters. This is not surprising for islanders. However, the quality of their dig out canoes have prevented them from venturing into the deep seas. The capacity of these canoes is also quite limited to two or three people. Even some of the dresses such as the bark belt on men is similar to the Jarawas except that it is narrower. They also wear leaf ornaments and nothing else. The men wear head bands made out of local materials. Some of the them paint their bodies in white clay. The dwellings are not elaborate and have even been seen to be sloping without any walls on the sides. Observations in 1965 and 1991 and subsequently after the tsunami gave an idea of the community which was staying a single place with a row of huts. The presence of multiple fire places suggested that these may have been shared by the families. They weave baskets made of cane and bamboo, which is mostly done by the women. The social hierarchy is believed to be in terms of powers vested with the elders with the communities following customary laws. The ritualistic practises are also not well known. Some experts point to the use of shells buried in places where death rituals occur. There are rituals for marriage and birth too. Pig skulls decorated with red colour are used as mark of trophy and seemed to be kept outside the hutments. There is no clarity whether they worship any deity or spirit. But this could not be ruled out. Artwork also remained scant and unnoticed in the dwellings. However, there were some markings made on their bows and arrows. There are believed to be some dance forms which are performed during rituals and celebrations. The tools and implements of the tribe are primarily bow, arrows and wooden harpoon spears for their hunting. The arrows are long and are used as spears too in their terrestrial hunting. The sharpening of blades is done by grinding and hammer stones. They also have plucking sticks to aid them in picking of fruits and nuts from dense vegetation and high trees. It is believed that metals like iron have been taken from those washed on the shores. Some of the utensils include bamboo pot and nautilus shells. The former for storing materials such as paints and the latter for keeping or bailing out waters from the canoes. Cane baskets are also made by weaving and are used for storage. The fishing nets are made of bark fibre threads with a cane rim and handle at the top. The resins oozing out of trees are burnt and used as a fragrance. During an expedition in 1990, even a chess board was found but this may have been washed ashore too. However, the tribe has to a large extent prevented any interface with outsiders and kept their civilisation isolation. Despite the acceptance of gifts from touring parties, they have not allowed anyone to establish a foothold. There have been incidents of fishermen being killed while entering the island. In an incident, even their bodies were not given as helicopters tried to recover it. They were met with bows and arrows. The aggressiveness has ironically been one of the traits that has preserved their culture. Maybe it has been fostered by the chequered history of the interactions. Starting from the British who actually came to the island and took some of them to Port Blair wherein some families died due to their lack of immunity to diseases.

The Onges

Onges

The **Onges** are another of the indigenous people who are believed to have come from Africa. They inhabit the Little Andaman island and at a point of time were also in Rutland. However, among all the tribes, they were probably the most affected due to the interaction with outsiders and settlements carried out in their territory. It all began with the Britishers who conquered the island in 1890. But the real effect came about in the 1960s when the forests were cleared for settlement. It confined the indigenous people to two places namely Dugong Creek and South Bay on their island. The tsunami of 2004 destroyed the latter and they all had to be relocated to Dugong Creek. Physiologically, they are Negroids with a short stature, broad face and nasal profile, peppercorn hair and scanty hair on their body. Among the indigenous people of the islands, they are the most adept at fishing and are known to venture into deep waters on account of their sturdy vessels. These canoes are made of a single tree trunk and fitted with out-riggers. It can carry a large number of fishermen. Their lifestyle is still about hunting, gathering and fishing. They gather fruits and nuts and hunt many animals ranging from wild boars and turtles. However, with the interaction with the settlers, they have come in touch with rice, wheat and tea. This has been the staple food of many of the Onges. Hunting is carried out with bows and arrows. Some of these are decorated with bark. In terms of their artisanal skills, they make mats, baskets and containers from cane and wood. These are used for storage of produce. The Kwalallu tree is used to make the containers for honey. The dwellings are made of tree trunks and canes. There are raised platforms supported by bamboo sticks with a wooden floor. Dogs and pigs are kept in the space below the floor. There are ceremonial dresses for men made out of bark. During ceremonies, men wear both dresses and waist belts. The women wear a fibrous tassel made out of the apex of a plant. This hangs over a string around the waist. Their social structure is divided into various patrilineal groups and marriage among the groups takes place. The social ritual for birth and death are about burying the placenta or the dead body at the place of the event. The marriage rituals are simple which include the bride sitting on the lap of the groom and embracing. The Onges believe in spirits and their existence on the land, water and sky. They worship them. Red paint is put on the body to keep off the evil spirits as well as protection against mosquitoes. Red ochre along with lard is smeared on the body during the mourning period since it is believed to ensure the existence of the soul after death. As indicated earlier, the settlement and deforestation of the island has affected the community. There were a number of developmental measures like provision of drinking water and groceries which has changed the overall lifestyle of the community. While many still practise hunting, gathering and fishing, the community is getting integrated into mainstream society. Even some of the other indigenous people like the Nicobarese have settled here.

The Great Andamanese

The Great Andamanese

The **Great Andamanese** are probably the first of the indigenous people who came to the islands. At one point of time, they occupied large swathes in the main islands of the Andamans. Today, they are confined only to the Strait Island and their numbers have drastically reduced to around 50. They are dark skinned, broad faced and have peppercorn hair. Their first encounter with the colonial powers was in 1789 when a British navy admiral Archibald Blair landed in the islands. However, in the interface with the colonial powers, the tribesmen were adversely affected primarily due to the loss of their forests and spread of diseases to which they had little immunity. The social customs include the practise of exogamy in marriage and nuclear families are the norm. The marriage ritual is elaborate with the groom sitting on the lap of the groom and both embracing each other. There is a traditional menu on the cards which includes tea and turtle meat. They believe in the after life spirits and have a long period of mourning for the dead. They worship a deity called Billikhu and are known to follow other religions. While some of them still practise hunting, gathering and fishing; there has been a wave of integration of the people into mainstream society with some of them even joining government service and working in plantations run by the government. Women also participate in the economic activities of the tribe and have the right of inheritance. The dwindling numbers have also led to re-organisation of the social hierarchy with the eldest being the de-facto chief who mediates within the tribe and with the government. With the interface with the settlers, their life has undergone a significant change. They are provided concrete house and power by the government with other social amenities. They trade products with the settlers and have lost much of their traditional culture. They are also politically active and participate in the elections. Once a thriving community, now they face the challenge of maintaining their culture in a rapidly changing world.

The Nicobarese

The Nicobarese

The **Nicobarese** are probably the most integrated indigenous people of the island chain. They embody a vibrant culture that thrives on agriculture and fishing, blending traditional practices with modern influences. They have Mongoloid features like the Shompens and are believed to have historically come from East Asia. Physiologically, they have a short stature with broad facial features. They inhabit many islands of the Nicobar and have also moved to the Andamans and mainland India for work. Their lifestyle which was primarily hunting, gathering and fishing has been significantly transformed. They have still managed to preserve some of their culture like music and dance. This is done during festive occasions. They live in modern concrete houses and have all the amenities of urban settlements. Many of them have excelled in specific activities including sports. They have excelled in professional road cycling. Many of them work outside the islands. They are probably the indigenous peoples of the islands who have been most integrated into mainstream society.

As one looks at all the indigenous people, it has been strangely one transgressing across the spectrum of complete isolation to full integration. On a scale across such a spectrum the sequence would be the Sentinelese, Shompens, Jarawas, Onges, Great Andamanese and finally the Nicobarese. All this points to the fact that the levels of development have been different. Some of these indigenous people have been more amenable to the acceptance of modernity while the others still want to preserve their way of life. It is a difficult call to understand as to which is the best model. However, the key aspect is that development has to have the right mixture of ensuring economic growth and preserving the cultural heritage and environment.

****

CHAPTER III

The Shompen Settlement

The eastern part of the Great Nicobar island houses a settlement of a few Shompens called Keyet. It was a picturesque surrounding with a dense forest cover. The beaches were rocky but gave a serene feeling since the waters were not choppy. There was abundance of flora and fauna in the rocky crevices as the cyclical tides controlled the ingress and outgress of water.

The settlement had around a score of adults and nearly the same number of children. There was a gender balance with both men and women having clear demarcation of work. The former were hunters who strayed deep into the forests to catch animals like wild boars, monkeys and lizards. Occasionally, they ventured out to catch even crocodiles in the swamps but this was risky. Fishing was restricted to the few water bodies and swamps but it provided them with a varied menu.

One of boys here was named Kayat. He had a family of six including his parents, grandparents and an elder sister. He had learnt the art of hunting taught by his father and grandfather down from the generations. Moreover, he also assisted his family in foraging for fruits and honey. The family also maintained a small farm growing yams and boy helped in tending to it. Whatever food was got was shared within the family as well as the settlement. Though there was no concept of a village elder, the seniors in the families took decisions.

Kayat was very smart and picked up all the nuances of hunting and foraging from his family quickly. The forests were like a homeground for him and slowly he learnt how to listen to noises for picking up the presence of animals. The chirping of birds and insects was an important aspect in this and the boy was adept at this art. There were times when he came so close to an unsuspecting boar or monkey that he could have just touched it. Moving with silence and stealth was something which had been ingrained in him as he learnt things very fast. After all it was a matter of survival for the Keyet. His skills in using the bow and arrow came from long sessions of practise back in his settlement. The aims were taken at nearby branches, leaves or stones. In due course, he became possibly the most skilful user of these tools in the community. He used these skills even to catch birds, one of the most difficult targets. And his success rate was significant. There came a time when the community took him to the hunting sessions just for these large birds, pigeons and pheasants.

He was also very adept in foraging for fruits and honey. The latter required a lot of skill since the honeybee sting could be painful. He knew the art of driving away the bees through smoke before taking their hive. Then he learnt to squeeze the maximum honey out of the hive. It was something taught to him over generations. But not everyone could pick it up with the ease that the boy did. His knowledge of the trees, shrubs, herbs and their produce was also exemplary. Moreover, he had a curiosity of the flora that none of his peers had. He was not afraid to check out new plants and what they hid beneath the cover. He had a knack of finding out if any of these had some poisonous substances lying beneath. It was both instinct and knowledge passed down over generations.

He also learnt to build the traditional homes from the materials available in the forest. Chiefly, this was bamboo, bark cloth, palm fronds and wood from the indigenous trees. This was probably the most difficult task of all the others. The right type of material had to be selected and cut into the precise shape required. The bamboo sticks had to be sturdy for bearing load as well not being sucked into the ground. Any openings had to be blocked to prevent insects getting inside. It required a lot of patience and hard work. Not many of his peers had the same level of dedication and concentration for this type of work. He assisted some of the others in his settlement too with the making of these homes.

With so much knowledge and dedication, he slowly became the Man Friday for the Keyet. He never shirked from taking on responsibility and additional work. But he was also a good team worker and co-ordinated well with peers to execute tasks such as hunting. Kayat also took care of the elderly and children in the community. After all the vulnerable section of the Shompen society required constant care with responsibility shared among all. The chores were about cleaning and feeding them as well as providing them any medical help and assisting the adult who was the medicine man in the community.

He had learnt the rigours of the tough life of the Shompens. He never complained and took all this in his stride. The others set him up as an example of virtuosity swelling the pride of his parents in the Keyet. However, could a person of his calibre and yearning for knowledge confine himself to a nomadic community bereft of the life that outsiders lived? Only time would tell.

****

CHAPTER IV

The Death

Finally, the status quo of being self-sustainable had to give way for the settlement. Not something that they desired but one that they could not avoid. After all the world outside them was developing at a breakneck speed. However, it is debatable as to whether this was for the better or worse.

It all began with one of the elderly men falling sick. The medicine man had virtually given up. One of the men then suggested that they make contact with the foreigners, as the outsiders were called in their local language. Some were not happy with the decision but since the condition was bad and the sick man was very popular in the settlement, they decided to try out this option.

The first dilemma was on how to contact the foreigners. They needed to move out of the dense forest and reach a forest guard house. It was a long trudge and the sick man had to be carried on a makeshift stretcher of bamboo. Kayat was singled out as one of the four Shompens who would carry this stretcher and make the trip. It was the boy's first venture out of the comfort of the woods. He had heard about the foreigners. Tales of how they lived a different lifestyle starting with their clothes. Then came the transport vehicles that they used and the things that they ate. But the boy had never seen anyone. There were butterflies in his stomach since he did not know what to expect. Some of the inhabitants of his settlement had said that these people were not trustworthy. Other said that they wanted to destroy the forests that his community lived in. There were other stories too of misbehaviour, giving edible things were which akin to poison and pilfering their works.

No wonder the boy was circumspect on the outcome of his mission. Anyhow, one of the four men knew the guard house and led the other three out of the forests. It was a difficult walk since the undergrowth was thick and there was little space to manoeuvre through it. The four had to cross rocky paths and carry the sick man over a rivulet that was in spate. There was an encounter with a family of boars but the animals were more scared of being hunted and scurried off.

Finally, they reached the guard house. However, the sentry was nowhere to be seen. The man who was leading them then let out a hoarse cry. And lo behold, two sentries came running to the guard house. They had sensed that it was the Shompen since this was their natural way of seeking help from the outsiders. Seeing the sick man on the stretcher, they quickly sensed the situation. One of them spoke the language and just reconfirmed it. Then they spoke on their walkie talkie and went over to get a four wheeler. There was a dirt road and the old man was placed at the back of the vehicle. The engine was started and the vehicle hummed into activity.

The boy was taken aback at all this. It was his first contact with the foreigners. The clothes that they wore looked strange. Both of them even had green caps and one of them was wearing a something made of glass with a frame over his eyes. They had worn shoes, which the boy had never seen before. He was admiring this attire and credibility of what he had heard before.

The jeep had only two additional places since both the guards had to sit in front. It was decided that the experienced Shompen and the boy would accompany the jeep and go to the town. The other two decided to go back to their settlements. When the jeep started to move, the boy was taken aback. He had never seen such a vehicle and wondered what it was. However, he was still gazing at the two guards who in a way seemed alien to him. He was basically absorbing the fact that the settlement seemed a totally different world from the two people he had just seen. The guards too were eyeing the boy since they had not seen someone this young from the tribee

The jeep did not seem comfortable for the boy from the start. It was a bumpy one and the vehicle rocked like one of the canoes did over choppy waters. The body literally shook and the sick man let out a cry. The driver realised this and slowed down the vehicle. But no sooner did he cover some distance, the natural instinct of speeding took over. Kayat despite all his physical prowess was taken aback at this rash driving. He felt the bumps and wondered how the sick man would be taking it. The old man realised the futility of letting out further cries of anguish. He in a way got used to the bumps and bore the pain just like he was bearing the pain of his ailment. The other Shompen was actually enjoying the ride by actually jumping in the jeep, with scant regard of the old man. The forest guards were amusement and encouraged him to do that.

As the vehicle made its way through the path in the dense growth, and then it met a road. It was a tarred road, black in colour which surprised the boy. He had never seen it before and immediately he could make out that the journey was smoother with the bumps having stopped. There was no feeling that they were riding a vehicle. Even the sick man was surprised and raised his head to see as to why the bumps had abruptly stopped. And the vehicle was going faster.

The vegetation around also changed and there were more open spaces. The boy was surprised to see the fields where some crops were being grown. There were some small hutments very much like their settlement which cropped up along the way. But they were much bigger and there were some cattle and dogs too around these. He saw some round shaped structures too like wells but did not understand what these were. Then suddenly the landscape changed as they entered a small town. There were small shops, vendors selling vegetables and fruits and then some sturdy houses too.

It was whole new world for the boy who once again had heard about it but it had never quite sunk in. He was mesmerised as if he had entered another civilisation so diametrically opposite his. The first feelings were of a chaotic environment around him. Vehicles honking, dogs barking, people calling each other, some crossing the road and many peering at the boy and his companion. The latter was the least surprising for him since he understood that the features of the Shompen was distinctly different from them. The sick man was woken up from his slumber in all this chaos. Probably the smooth ride on the tarred road had calmed his nerves and he dozed off.

Finally, they reached a large building and the vehicle went inside. It was a hospital but Kayat had little idea. It was more chaotic than the market place he saw. Overcrowded and he could see that many of them appeared sick as they moved slowly. Others were accompanying them and some of them even had those white colour bandages. He instantly understood that this was a place where sick people like the old man came. The other guard then motioned them to stay in the vehicle and went inside the building. He came out in some time and asked them to accompany him. The other Shompen understood the language but Kayat knew nothing. However, he was smart enough to pick up the tone and the gestures made. They carried the old man on the stretcher and went inside. The interiors seemed a bigger mess that the outside of the building. The boy was shocked at the sheer number of people. There were some people wearing white clothes which instantly related to him as people who would cure ailment. Much like medicine man but with white clothes on.

Finally, the man was transferred to a bed which was on wheels. This was more comfortable than the bamboo stretcher on which he had come. He was then taken to a room where both the Shompens were asked to wait outside. The guard who had accompanied in was the translator since he was conversant with the language. Outside it was a queue of people and they were all observing the two like some museum specimen. Looking at their faces, bare bodies and the loin cloth. Some of them were laughing which made the two uncomfortable. Even the hospital staff were peering at them but they managed to get them two seats to sit. After all they did not want the situation inside the hospital to become unmanageable. They also had to rebuke the patients and their attendants to take their gaze off the two.

Kayat was experiencing this for the first time and became very uncomfortable. The other Shompen who had experienced this earlier put his hand around him and asked him to relax. "*These people are not used to us. You see the clothes they wear and how different it is from us. Don't we also look so different from them.*" It was then that the boy understood all this curiosity. However, with time he was not flustered by all this attention. It was just amusing and it gave him a perspective of how these people and his tribe lived in possibly two different worlds. Some children in the crowd came up to them and in all their innocence just touched them. The other Shompen wasn't having any of this triviality. He gave a stern look to the children in order to scare them away. The first reaction of Kayat was to remove their hand but he gave a smile. He was always fond of them back in the tribe too since he had the responsibility of looking after some of them. However, some of the parents or relatives of those children asked them to come back. They said something to their kids. Though the boy did not understand the language, he could make out that it was something unpleasant said about them which made the children shirk and run back. It was his first emotion of mistrust and Kayat felt strange about it.

Nevertheless, it was not the time to focus on these things. The old man was being treated and they were waiting for some news. Unfortunately, after an hour, the guards came rushing out. They seem to be in panic. When asked, they mentioned that they had to go to get some medicines and both rushed out. They came back within a few minutes with a large cover and they went in again to the room. A doctor also came rushing into the room in some time. Both the Shompens were sure that there was something not right and it was to do with the old man. The latter was anyway in a poor condition and the journey was also exhausting.

No sooner were their thoughts wandering that the guards came out very solemnly. They had to break the news that the old man was no more. The smart boy understood it before any word was uttered. The other Shompen nevertheless conveyed the message to Kayat as the guards tried to comfort both of them. They went inside and saw a large room with many beds. It was crowded and there was a rush of people up and down. The old man was lying on one of the beds with his body covered in white cloth. There were some contraptions like a drip and medicines kept on a table next to the bed. There was a doctor who conveyed something which neither of them understood but nodded. The other patients were curiously looking at the Shompens. Nothing different from their experience in the waiting hall of the hospital. Since the two had got used to this unwarranted attention, there were more at comfort here. The moment was also solemn as the body of the old man lay in front of them. Both of them shed a tear but then calmed themselves. One of the forest guards then told them to wait outside and he would return after completing the formalities.

The wait was fairly long. Little did the two Shompens understand the reasons for this delay. They had no inkling of the paperwork required for all this. After all it was a case of death and hence the formalities were more rigorous. Finally, the guards came out after a long wait. They had wheeled the dead body and the boy and his companion helped them to take it out of the hospital Everyone's eyes were glued on the stretcher and the two indigenous people as they moved to the exit and into the parking premises. The body was removed from the stretcher and placed at the back end of the van. The guards offered some food but the two did not eat. It was a period of mourning for them. However, the guards took time to eat as they were famished.

The boy took the time to survey the place. Kayat could see that a number of trees were less, ostensibly cut to make way for open spaces. The place was also dirty with a lot of litter strewn around. There was a lot of noise and chaos with vehicles of all hues ranging for cycles to motorised ones vying for the limited space. It hit him a bit hard from the serenity and peace of his forest abode. The feeling was a bit unpleasant. However, he could see that people had clothes to wear and more things to eat. But he still had the elements of doubt as to whether all this worth the trade off with the green environment back home. The other Shompen could see the boy's intense gaze. But he chipped in, "*This place is great. People have all the amenities. They work and their children learn so many things in a school. Wish I could come here sometime*". Albeit, the boy was not so sure.

However, the word "*school*" struck a chord. He enquired from the other Shompen about it. The other man mentioned that it was a place where people sent their children to learn. Kayat instantly became curious. Nearing twenty, it did not seem the right time to think about school. But the boy was always yearning to learn new things. The forests had broadened his horizon but with the passage of time he felt that there was nothing more to digest. The elders had given him all the requisite information that they knew. He had explored things on his own and learnt a lot, even through mistakes. Which plant to avoid, what sounds to look out for, how to tackle a dangerous encounter with a family of wild boars or a crocodile etc? Now he felt that a school, whatever it was, would satiate his appetite for information.

When the guards came back, he instantly blurted out that he wanted to go to school. While one of the guards burst out laughing, the other became inquisitive. He wanted to understand the reason for this demand. Kayat said tersely, "*I want to learn new things*". The other guard instantly retorted, "*What do you want to learn?*". The boy thought for some time and said, "*Whatever the school teaches that I don't know about.*" He was impressed with this answer. After all, none of the tribesman had made such a request before. The boy seemed smart in his interactions too. He could see that despite the initial discomfort which was natural, the boy was not fazed by all the people staring at him and the other Shompen. He seemed brave and quite comfortable in such a large gathering. He responded saying that he would talk to people about this.

However, now it was not the time for them to ponder over schooling. They had to return with the body. The tribesman had a ritual of burying the body in a grave. Tradition demanded that a pig had to be caught and killed. Kayat had seen this once and did not like the idea of an animal sacrifice. But then he had to respect the tradition. He also remembered that once they had moved from the location where the death had occurred. Probably, it was a sign that the place was not conducive for living.

The body was placed on leaves and on the stretcher. The forest guards had arranged for all that since they were well aware of the tradition of the Shompens. The journey began as the four people in the vehicle were in a sombre mood. They were all anxious as no one could predict the response of the elders in the village. Would they stick to their traditions since this death was not in the village. It was a foreign land. Would they get angry and retaliate, probably against the forest guards. However, Kayat was clear that this was unlikely since the two forest men had helped out the community so much. Moreover, the old man was in a precarious condition and most of the villagers did not have any hope of his survival. They agreed to send him out just to see if he could be saved. But this was indeed the first death outside the community and the man was well respected. Having lived in the wild, even the boy was aware that there was an element of unpredictability in the behaviour of his kinsmen. Sometimes, he also felt that he too lacked the power to gauge his own response to any situation. The vagaries of nature had probably constructed this behavioural response.

The return journey was as bad as the one they had undertaken. The mood was sombre since they were carrying a dead body back home. The boy did look up to see his environment but did not have the same level of curiosity. The only thing that he seemed more interested was a group of children in the same coloured set of clothes coming out of a building. On enquiry, he was told that this was a school where parents sent their children to learn. This aroused him and Kayat was looking intently at the children coming out of the building. They had a bag on their backs and some of them were walking back with their friends. They too gazed at the Shompens given their different looks. Some of them shouted at them more like children surprised at seeing someone out of the ordinary. The two of them just smiled back and did not respond. It was the occasion that got to them and they did not want to take a break and interact with the children. The guards gave some dirty looks to the children to keep them being more inquisitive. They had no plans to stop the vehicle and sped away from the school. One of the guards told the boy, "*I will get you here some day since you are interested. But be prepared for these children to stare at you.*" Kayat replied, "*That would only be in the beginning. I will cope up with that*". The man was impressed with the answer and decided that he would help the boy once all this got over. He knew that the government had built some schools only for the indigenous people and hence interaction with foreigners was not needed. He told this to the boy, who had mixed feelings on this. While he seemed happy at other children not staring at them, Kayat was also aware that this might prevent them from socialising with the outsiders and understand them better.

Soon the vehicle reached the forest house. The latter part of the journey was difficult since the track was a dirt one and the vehicle had to wind its way through. It was bumpy and the tribesmen were not used to it. However, the boy had experienced it once and he was ready for it. Once they reached the destination, it was time to place the body on the bamboo stretcher and walk. They took a small break in the forest house and had some water and some light snacks. The guards got some other items for the cremation like some oil, candles, matchbox and some religious items like thread and cloth. Then the four of them carried the body into the settlement. It was a difficult journey since all of them were tired after the drive. Moreover, there was anxiety on what would be the reception at the settlement. The boy was praying that the villagers should not vent out their anger at the guards who were only there to help. After a taxing trek through the woods, they reached the settlement. Kayat had studied their journey well and knew the route better than the other Shompen. Even the guards were surprised since it was the other man who was more experienced and this boy was pointing to areas and naming some landmarks they passed. After reaching the destination, the boy called out to the elders and they all came. One of the elders asked them and the instant reply of the boy was "*He died peacefully in the town*". This was a more pragmatic reply which even surprised the other Shompen. He had planned to break the news in a more apologetic manner like "*We couldn't save him*", but Kayat had already done the ground work. He had to calm the possible frayed nerves of his kinsmen.

The elder to whom the news was broken went into a semi-shock. Despite the ailing condition of the man, they did not expect this news, probably given the confidence level of the treatment outside. Some of the men became angry. "*What did they do with him in the town? Couldn't they look after him? What was the use of sending him outside. We could have cared for him here and saved him.*" The medicine man seemed to be the happiest at the development. They targeted their anger at the two guards who understood that the situation could get ugly. While the other Shompen kept quite, the boy sensed the mood and intervened. "*They did their best but the condition of our elder was very bad. They had beds, medicines and so many people to take care of him. But all this could not save him.*" The men were in no mood to listen to all this. They were angry. However, one of the elders intervened and stopped the others. "*What the boy says is true? The man was in bad shape and didn't have much time left. We sent him to the town as the measure of the last resort. Atleast they tried their best to save him.*" Kayat nodded in defence of the man.

It was only then that the situation became calm. The guards were surprised at the young boy speaking out. He had not seen the treatment given in the room of the hospital. Moreover, the ride was bumpy and the old man would have been discomforted by it. The entire environment of the hospital would also have been cultural shock for him. Such a crowded and a chaotic look would have surprised any outsider. And yet he was trying to come to the rescue of the guards by calming the situation. He handled it with maturity much beyond his age. This was highly impressive. And he even wanted to go to school and learn new things. There was something about Kayat that impressed the guards. One of them thought, "*This boy is destined for bigger things outside his community.*"

So the guards breathed a sigh of relief as they planned to head back. The elder requested them to stay and be part of the cremation. It was a sign that they were part of the larger community since they were helping them out. It was a sudden change in the situation which could have got very volatile. With the things they had got, a simple ceremony was held. All the families got together. Tears were shed as the man was an elder who was respected in the settlement. The body was placed on the ground in front of an old tree. A grave was dug and some leaves placed in it. Some prayers were said by the elders as the families cried. They went around touching the dead man's forehead. Finally, the body was placed in the grave and one final set of prayers were said. It was then covered with mud. Some flowers were placed on the ground above.

However, the hardest part of all this was that the elders decided to move the settlement from where it was. This was a ritual done by the tribe. However, it was normally done when one of their kin died in the settlement. The reason is believed to be that of the spirits residing in the area after death as well as the place itself being a bad omen. This case was however different as the old man had died outside the forests in a hospital. Nevertheless, no one wanted to take a stand contrary to tradition. Some did point out to this fact but no one stuck their neck out. It was an easy decision for the elders. An easy decision for them but having larger repercussions since they had to shift lock stock and barrel to a new place. Not many envied redoing all the hard work of removing all the material and relocating. It would take atleast a few days for the entire shifting to take place. The boy also remembered the time when he and some of his peers had to construct a house since one of the women was about to give birth. They had to create the special hut since she would be relocated there till the birth and a few subsequent days. After that the future of that hut was not sure and it was in disarray since no one used it and there was no other birth for a long time. No one was allowed to go to that place too.

So no sooner did the dust settle down on the burial ritual, the guards decided to leave. Before that one of them asked the elder permission to allow the boy to join school. The elder was surprised at this request and called for the boy and his father. He was initially taken aback but then gathered his wits. When probed, Kayat responded *"I want to join and understand new things. I saw so many buildings, markets and places that there is a new world out there. While I love our forests, it would be good to understand other things of which we know little about"*. The elder was also taken aback at this response. Some of the others who overheard the conversation were smirking at what the boy had said. But the former was impressed. He too had harboured the ambition of moving out of the settlement and see the other side of the world. But his parents and family had dissuaded him. Now he did not want this boy to face the same fate. For good or for bad, he wanted someone from the village to see the other side and tell all back home about it. But knowing the difficult times ahead during relocation, he responded to the guard, "*Let him first help us relocate to the new place. Then we will see.*" The guard was experienced enough to read between the lines. He knew by the tone of the response that this was an assent. He thanked the elder and offered to help in the relocation too. After all, how could they miss an opportunity to have good relations with the indigenous people of the forests that they administered. The elder reciprocated this gesture and agreed for the help. This despite some frowns from other adults who did not want other people helping them out with building the new houses. But the elder knew that the guards had some tools which would be of immense help.

Finally, the guards went back and returned after some time with some tools. Hammers, chisels, knives and some nails. The boy looked at these with wonder. The location of the new site had already been made and it was not very far from where they were living. This too had a water source which was the same rivulet slightly upstream. After all water was a precious commodity in these parts. Most of the existing structures were removed and the entire community was involved in the transportation. Apart from the existing material, pandanus and cane were used in the making of the huts which were built on stilts. Even bamboo was used as a material for making mattresses and pillow. The entire community lent a hand in this venture. The guards helped to the extent they could. Instead of making huts, they focussed the work on clearing the forests and making an open area for placing the huts. After all, each family wanted to tailor the huts as per their desires and any intrusion in this would not been seen in a proper light.

The entire exercise took a couple of days. During this time the guards went back and forth to their forest house. The community fed them with whatever they made. It was complete teamwork as the division of work was clear. Each person ranging from men, women and grown up children worked like clockwork to complete the assigned task. The greatest effort was required in the hut of the elder since it also doubled up as one for visitors, both from other villages and outsiders to stay, if needed. The forest guards were actively involved in this activity. It was a collective exercise at the end of which the new settlement had come up. All the finishing touches could be given only in due course of habitation.

After this assignment was complete, the guards took their leave. It was a warm send off for all the efforts they put in. The best of food was served starting with pork, fish, rice and traditional dish made of the pandanus fruit. They all ate heartily since they were all famished after the strain of relocation. It has been one good teamwork and increased the camaraderie between the tribesmen and the outsiders.

Within a few days, one of the guards returned and told the elder that he had talked about the school. There was one a few kilometres away which had been opened specially for the Shompens but no one had come. It was in the forests but in the territory of another of the communities. They needed two children from this community and would take others from elsewhere. The elder remembered all this conversation and asked the guards to be comfortable in his hut. He soon returned with Kayat and another child. The latter was not keen but the elder had influenced his parents who could not refuse. The boy was particularly happy to see the guard and knew at once that it was about the school. Both the set of parents were not very happy about their children going to such a far off place and in the hands of outsiders. Their greater concern was about their absence for lending a helping hand for the chores of the household. However, they gave in to the pressure.

****

CHAPTER V

The School

It was a good hour trek in the forests to the school. Kayat had never been to these parts of the woods. There was a general cautionary warning to all his peers about the risk of moving out of the comfort of their land. There was the danger of both adversial tribesmen as well as outsiders. There had been some clashes between different clans and the stories of these scared many. Some of these were bloody even leading to loss of lives. These clashes occurred with both their own kin, the Shompens and with the other tribes, the Nicobarese. However, Kayat had that adventure streak in him and the all the dangers did not deter him. Once upon a time the boy had attempted to enlist his peers for an adventure outside their forests but no one wanted to take on this risk. Hence, he went alone on a long walk but ended up reaching a beachhead that was deserted. The calmness of the sea with the splashing of the blue waters against a white sandy shore had enticed him to spend a good amount of time there. There were times when the tribesmen had taken him to the other beaches but this was for the first time that he was on his own thinking and dreaming. Basically, the adventure spirit was ingrained in him though he well understood the perils of overstepping the limits in wilderness that they dwelt. He was cognisant of the dangers in these forests. It was akin to the vagaries of nature. Hence, he was pragmatic in what he did and controlled this adventurous streak if the circumstances so demanded.

The forests were dense as the three made their way to the school. It seemed that the guard was well versed with the topography as he led the way. There was a small pathway but the shrubbery had masked it in certain places. He had to use a stick to clear the overgrowth. There was the danger of wild animals including snakes, so the walk was slow. The two boys, who had grown up in the forests were more adept at sensing danger. Kayat sent a cautionary note when he heard some noises. "*That's the hissing of a snake, don't touch that plant*", he told the guard at one point. They encountered some monkeys who were actually scared of probably being hunted and scooted away. Finally, after a good hour of brisk walking, they reached a building, fairly dilapidated. Something was written on the front but neither boys could read. The guard explained that this was a school made for the indigenous tribes but had not been used. Hence the condition was bad.

However, compared to their own huts, the structure seemed sturdy.

The three of them went inside to examine the building. There were some chairs and desks in rooms with a blackboard. The boys had not seen such a structure and were gazing at it in amazement. They were not sure of the purpose but the boy could slowly understand that this would be the place where they would need to sit and be taught by someone. There was a tap with running water and this was indeed heartening to see. There were toilets, though not in good condition. It seemed more hygenic than relieving yourself in the woods.

However, the rooms were empty and they looked around. Apart from the chairs, there were some drawings put up on the wall, a blackboard which the boys saw for the first time with a table just in front of that. Then suddenly an elderly man with spectacles came to the room. The boys were startled more by what he wore over the eyes. This aroused their curiosity and although the boy did see some people with the same contraption in the hospital, he did not particularly take notice due to the gravity of that situation where the old man was battling for his life. The man immediately understood what the boys were thinking and responded to them in their language. "*My eyesight is weak and hence I am using this thing known as spectacles. It improves your vision. I am your teacher and will take classes so that you understand about the world around you. The other students from the settlements are also coming.*" The two boys were surprised and became inquisitive. The teacher showed up how to sit in the chair and asked them to do so. They were initially reluctant but then took their places sharing one of the desks. They had never encountered a public place and had not interacted with outsiders. Hence the diffidence. The man barring his complexion seemed was talking very much like an elder of the Keyet.

No sooner had he said this that many other children from different settlements came into the school. They too seemed to have trudged a long way through the forests to reach here. He recognised some of them having the same physical characteristics as him. However, there were others who were of a lighter complexion and seemed smaller in size. He could make out these physiological differences and wondered if these were also foreigners. Kayat then remembered the encounter with the Nicobarese in the dense forests on one of his trips. It was adversial and an unpleasant situation as both sides almost came to blows with their arrows and spears. It was only with the intervention of the elders on both sides, including the man who had died in the town, that saved the situation. Kayat had interacted with some of his peers too from that tribe. He could only make out some words that they spoke but could communicate with home hand gestures. He had some other encounters too with that tribe too. These were nevertheless more pleasant and in those conversations had picked up the language. Kayat was a fast learner and had a knack of learning a new tongue.

The boy could thus distinguish the third category of people who were the outsiders. For example the guards who were considered in the category were much darker in complexion. Almost all the people in the hospital that he had gone taking the old man had the same dark complexion. Even among these, there were some people who had nearly the same complexion as themselves. Their teacher was one such but the eyes of these outsiders were different from both the tribal communities. It was something that Kayat was curious about and slowly imbibed. A forest dweller who had not seen life beyond the confines of his community was slowly assimilating the cultural hues around him. The global village was being pryed open in front of him and he was eager to learn more.

It was a motley group of around ten children in the room. All in the same age group as Kayat with some of his tribe. The man motioned them to sit and they all did. Another person was there with the instructor and he wore a dress of natural material as the boys. They recognised him to be part of one of their tribes. Soon he introduced himself as a headman of a settlement and said that he would translate if the boys could not comprehend what was being said. The kids were all curious about what would be told to them.

The teacher then began by showing the class some pictures of different tribes of the region. Probably, he did not want to dive into the usual alphabets and numbers class. Maybe it would have disinterested the group. He showed them the pictures of the main tribes in the region just to acquaint them with the cultural milieu of the land. He began with a map showing the various islands of Andaman and Nicobar. The other man translated what the teacher said. It was an eye opener for the students. Initially, they all giggled hesitant to ask anything. But slowly with some coaxing from the translator, the boy stood up and asked, "*How can we go up there to the topmost island and how much time does it take?*". The teacher then responded stating that journey is long and if we take the canoes that the tribes used, it would take many days of non-stop rowing including in the night. All the boys were surprised at the large expanse of the islands. He further mentioned that there were large vessels which could cover this distance in less than a day. He then showed the picture of one of these liners that transported passengers. The picture was passed one by one to all the boys and they were overawed by the size and the inner décor where there were seats. It began sinking into them that their forests were indeed a very small part of the entire ecosystem around.

The teacher did not want to prescribe anything and allowed the flow of thoughts. He used the pictures available and even the videos on his phone to explain many things about the islands. The boys were surprised to see a mobile phone for the first time and the many videos in it. It was indeed a shock after living in the dense woods with little idea of the technologies available. The teacher first concentrated on the Great Nicobar explaining its flora and fauna. This caught the interest of the boys as he talked about the number of snake species, the types of crocodiles, insects in the wild, species of birds etc. It was all quite familiar to them but yet someone explaining these in detail was a different proposition altogether. The plant species were also dwelt at length and the master explained them with pictures to make it more interesting. It was an eye opener for many children who had not ventured deep into woods for hunting.

After all this, there was a well earned break. The children were given some biscuits and milk. It was a pleasant surprise. The boy felt that it did not taste as good as the pandunus fruit but it had a different sweet tinge to it. The milk was also different from the raw cattle milk that they were used to. But with the school providing these refreshments, the boys felt energetic for the next session. It was also a means of socialising and the boy talked to some other classmates. They spoke in the same language since they were from his tribe. It was the usual questions about family members and their pastimes.

Some of the children were from the other tribe, the Nicobarese. It was clear that they stayed closer to the shores and were not aware of the flora and fauna of the land. Neither were they into hunting and foraging in the forests. One of the boys, names Tibo chatted with the boy. The language was different but with the experience that Kayat had gained in his earlier encounters with the other tribe enabled him to communicate. It was a mixture of sign language and some words which seemed similar. Tibo on the other hand was also a smart lad and quickly latched onto the communication channel. After the break, the two decided to sit next to each other and continue their comical conversation interspersed with gestures.

The other boys were surprised that the two had decided to take adjacent seats. The class was otherwise clearly demarcated between the two tribes.

Five from each and occupying the two ends of the class. Apart from these two boys, all seemed to be in their own tribal group. Probably a bit reticent to break the ice with the other on account of the different languages. The teacher could sense this but he did not want to break them from their comfort zone. After all it was the first day and it would take time for the inter-mingling.

The next session proceeded to one of questions and answers on the various pictures and videos shown. There was that initial hesitancy since, not uncommon in a school environment. But slowly with some prodding from the elder, the kids spoke out and tried to provide answers. Tibo was smart and was able to answer many questions. He impressed the teacher. Kayat, also made his points and it was clear that the two boys were in a different zone from the rest. Not only was there a zest for learning but they seemed to be very keen to learn new things about their land. The elder, who was a Shompen, also joined in the conversation and provided his wealth of knowledge gathered over the years. At one point of time, there was also a reference to the conflicts between the two tribes. He recounted an incident when the two sides were all ready to attack each other with spears and bows. Then suddenly a pig charged between them, probably out of fright. And the frontline warriors on both sides broke into a laugh. It was amusing and the animal, normally their kill, had managed to stop a potentially dangerous fight. The boys all laughed heartily as if was a fairy tale. This comical story not only had the class gel but it sent a message to the boys that all these fights may very well be an exercise in futility. It was probably better to live in harmony.

But one key difference the students learnt about the tribes was their assimilation to mainstream society. It was told by the teacher that the Nicobarese had integrated well into mainstream society. They were working with the settlers and even doing jobs. Tibo's community was a small one that still did not want to leave their forest abode and integrate. It seemed that the elders had chosen the path. However, it is the kin of these elders who had now decided to send their children to this school. Hence some of the others in the community were not very happy about all this and resisted any schooling for their children. Tibo himself mentioned to Kayat that his cousins were living in urban settlements and he was once taken to a hospital there. Kayat asked him about the reason and the boy just responded, "*Don't know what it is but sometimes I get fever and feel weak. None of the local herbs have been able to treat me. But even the hospital in my cousins place gave me something to eat but it did not work."*

The teacher continued this informal method of teaching without really taxing the boys. After all, it was their first day and it was important to get them interested. The exercise continued until lunch where a sumptuous offering was made. It was a mixture of pandunus fruit, rice and pork. All the children ate heartily since they were hungry after all these classes. Then it was time for a sport. The game of Kabaddi was chosen with the rules explained. It was not easy since many of these kids had not indulged in these outdoor activities in their settlements. The elder who himself had not played much tried his best to explain the nuances of the game. Nevertheless, with some effort and actual play by the two elders, the game was explained. With no equipment, the game had to be a purely physical one and hence the particular sport was chosen. All the various aspects of the game, holding of the breadth, attacking the opposition on both flanks, use of the leg kick, co-ordination of the defence to thwart the attackers, grabbing of the legs and ensuring that if the attacker manages to escape, the others must keep themselves out were all explained. It was not easy but the children started playing. It was a golden opportunity for the children of the two tribes, living apart in the forests to communicate on their strategy. It was not easy with the disparity in the languages but they made an effort. It was obvious as to who would be made the captains. The two boys who had developed a good friendship and were actively involved in the lessons taught were the two main protagonists. All the kids had a great time and no one cared as to which team one. They established a camaraderie like nothing else could. It was for the first time that the two new friends also understood the power of sport for creating a bond. The teacher and the elder were thrilled at the outcome of the sport. They all ended on a high note as all the students left for their settlements.

The next school was held after a couple of days. All the boys looked forward to it. With the positive feedback given by them back home, there was further enthusiasm and this time fifteen of them turned up. The elders were clearly divided on this. Having brought up in the traditional way of life, many were suspicious of foreign influence. For them, it would ruin their way of life and make their children pick up the bad habits and probably leave their settlements. The latter was not far from the truth. However, some others realised that they needed to live with their neighbours in peace and interaction was inevitable. Getting their children to understand all this was considered by them as a good way out.

Both Kayat and Tibo were happy to meet each other again. Since both of them had come in early, there was some time to chat up. The teacher and the elder had already reached the premises but they intentionally did not want to go directly to class. Another person from the other tribe was also part of the teaching entourage today given the size of the students. It was a plan to provide time to socialise and in the process learn to communicate. Both the boys were not staying very far off in terms of geographical distance on the island but the settlements avoided each other. There was a history of territorial conflicts and the boys were also sucked into this political maelstrom. However, the school was a good opportunity for them to so called "*network*" and socialise. The language was a barrier but the Shompen boy had picked up some nuances of Andamanese. It was a mixture of sign language and some words but the key part was that the message was being conveyed. Tibo also tried to learn the language of his friend but he found it harder. Thus the communication was being established in one of the languages. It was a good half an hour of socialising time for the class. Some of them chose to observe the surroundings since they were new. A few tried to talk to each other but only within the tribe. It was only these two who broke that barrier across the two communities. During this encounter, Kayat saw that Tibo was weak. He touched his forehead and felt the fever. The teacher reached out to a box and gave the boy a medicine but it did not seem to work. "*The fever will go down in some time. But I keep getting it off and on*", Tibo said.

The talk related to the residence, families, lifestyles and the usual teenage chatter. It was a way of learning to communicate as well as understand each other's cultures. It was clear that both the boys were smart and were willing to go out of the way to socialise. It seemed that both of them took up the task of going to school with the purpose of learning aspects beyond their narrow community boundary. They also tried to get others to talk to each other across the tribes. But the language was the stumbling block for many. Others did not want to be seen talking to strangers outside their community. There were those cautionary tales from elders of how they much keep to themselves and protect their community from foreigners.

Then the teacher came in with the two elders to take the class. He welcomed some of the new children and inquired about the others. The new ones introduced themselves with some still shy of speaking to outsiders. Nevertheless, the elders too goaded them to speak. Every statement of the teacher was translated by the two elders. Their presence also comforted some of the students. This time the class was on the entire region of Andaman and Nicobar islands. Information was provided through pictures of the other tribes. Their culture, features, occupation, settlement, food and the way of life. It was an eye opener for the students. The vastness of their land and the diversity what was hit them. Some of them were keenly looking at the pictures of the other tribesmen, tribeswomen and their children. They had no idea of the people living in the other forests of their land. Some of the landscapes shown were also stunning and they were mesmerised by the beauty of their land. Many had not seen the pictures of the blue waters of the oceans or the beaches. They never knew that such a world existed far away from their communities. Even the wealth of the flora and fauna of the forests were new to some as they had not seen all of these despite being part of the hunting entourages of their communities.

However, the most interesting story for them was that of the Sentinelese tribe. It was told that they lived in an isolated island of North Sentinel and had little contact with the outside world. Stories of them attacking a stranded ship was an interesting snippet which got the children interested. They were keen to know about the tribe but not much was known about them. Questions that were posed were about their homes, eating habits, what the children did, way of life etc. It was in a way getting to know about the culture of the islands. The pictures and some videos literally brought this right in front of the eager pupils.

The two new found friends showed a special interest in the geography of the islands starting from the southern most island where they all lived to the North Andaman. They were looking up each of the islands trying to understand the distance and size. The studied the water bodies that separated them including the ten degree channel, the Sombrero channel, Duncan passage and the Coco channel. It was as if they were trying to find out the best route to traverse the entire chain. They were also keen to know about all the indigenous tribes and the islands where they lived.

Time passed so fast that the break came. All of the students then went to have their snacks. It was time to imbibe all they had learnt. It was just the second day but the content taught was something they had no clue about. The new students were busy savouring the milk and biscuits served. It was a surprising change from their usual diet and hence the curiosity. The two boys also relished the snack and went out for having a chit chat. Nothing like letting your thoughts wander in the outdoors. They too were stunned by what they heard about North Sentinel and its enigmatic denizens who refused contact with the outside world. It was in those fleeting moments that the adventure spirit in them arose. Did they really want to go to that island? Not sure, but then curiosity was definitely aroused. Just like kids, the questions arose. If they go there, would they be killed? Could they meet kids of their own age among the Sentinelese and get them back from that island? Can they communicate with them?

So the school days went on and on. It was not regular and neither were children the same. Some communities preferred to send their kids in rotation so that everyone got covered. Others stopped them from going when they were required for some work at home. The classes also varied and other subjects were also taken up. There was some common interested generated on Bollywood films and music as stories were explained to the students. With the age categories varied, it was difficult to have any particular syllabus to be taught. A lot of patience was required with language being the major barrier. The focus was on spoken skills and followed by some reading ones. It was too difficult to get into the writing skills. Moreover, the education had to be pragmatic for the children especially for life in the community. After all, it was not envisaged that these children would relocate from their communities. There was thus no need to simple ape the existing educational curriculum which had a different premise.

CHAPTER VI

The Conspiracy

The schooling went on intermittently. However, it provided both Kayat and Tibo the opportunity to meet. Once during their rendezvous, they decided to travel outside their communities to meet. Both had a good idea of the direction from school and with instinct could find out the way from their communities. The two issues were the dense forest with the uncertain dangers of wild animals and the reluctance of the village elders to allow them to travel. However, these were trivial for the adventure fuelled boys.

They decided a particular day and time for the rendezvous midway from the two settlements. It was too risky to come to the others settlement since a person appointed by the elder would be on guard. So they had to find an excuse to venture without any suspicion. One of the obvious reasons was to go out for fetching plants from the forest. The boys were too young to hunt alone and hence hunting could not be an alibi. Both the boys thus manage to leave their settlement on the appointed day and time.

Kayat had to navigate the denser vegetation and hence was slowed down by the thick shrubbery. Tibo on the other hand had an easier passage since a worn down pathway was there. Nevertheless, the place was always swarming with snakes which could be a danger. Wild boars could also be unpredictable with their charging, if they felt threatened. Both the boys used all their experience of the dense woods to navigate the path. The rendezvous point was a clearing in the woods which had lesser dangers. The only catch was that elders from the community could catch them if they were around that areas during hunting. Fortunately, none of that happened. Yet life in the woods had taught them be circumspect.

Both were happy to meet each other. Tibo had made the trip despite having a fever and related weakness. This had become part of his life and he hoped for some cure. It was their first experience of having left their dwellings without informing about the secret rendezvous. It was the usual boy talk as the two had not met for a long time in school. Sharing of experiences and some incidents in their settlements. Living amidst the lap of wild nature, there was always something unexpected. A great hunting catch, injuries to the hunters and their treatment, visits or skirmishes from other settlements etc. This time it was about the birth of a child in the

Nicobarese settlement. It was a boy and there was celebration in the settlement. Tibo had lent a hand in the construction of the hut where the mother stayed with some women elders who also acted as midwives. In the Shompen settlement, it was about one of the young men catching a crocodile on his own. It was always a dangerous hunt since the animal had an advantage in the water. It was a rare feat and everyone applauded the young man. A crocodile had not been caught in the settlement for a long time and everyone cherished the dish that was cooked.

The communication was much smoother as the Shompen boy seemed well conversant with Nicobarese. They also discussed school and how it had opened up a whole new world for them. The information on the various tribes of the land and the outsiders was discussed. It was then that the boys decided to venture out on their own to see this world. It was the story of the Sentinelese which probably was the most interesting to the two. Kayat was the first to blurt out, "*Lets explore that island.*". Tibo was a bit circumspect with a response, "*Are you mad? First of all how will be reach to a place so far off? Even if we manage, they are hostile and would kill us.*" They thought about it for some time. Then the Shompen boy responded, "*Fine, let us first try to meet the other tribes and see the response. Then we can decide whether it is worth taking the risk.*" Tibo was not so sure especially with his ailment. So they let the moment pass.

The two then explored other parts of the forest trying to look for animals and plants. They spotted some monkeys who ran away in fear, but hunting was not in their agenda. It was more about understanding the woods and its dangers. After all their decision entailed them to go into unchartered woods and meet these indigenous people. Picking up sounds was an essential part of this exploration. After all stealth was a key part of hunting and obviating danger. It would stand them in good stead for the perilous journey ahead. A bold decision had been taken by the boys and now they needed to be well prepared for it.

There was another rendezvous which the two decided during one of the school sessions. The plan was to meet in the dense forests and then make their way to the sea shore. They managed to reach the beach head with the Shompen boy leading the way. It was a difficult walk through the forests. The experience was enriching since Tibo had never ventured alone like this. They had to look out for danger based on the sounds and smell. The sea was part of the life of the Nicobarese and they even went fishing into the shallow waters. They watched the hitting of the waves on the shore and was mesmerised. It was peaceful and so different from the lurking dangers of the dense forest. No sounds or smell to worry about, just relaxing. Tibo then said, "*while the sea may be calm, venturing into it is as dangerous as the forest. One never knows how the water will behave. There have been cases when the fishing canoe have drowned and the sturdy men on it could not save themselves in the rough waters. Just like we listen to sounds in the forests, we need to gauge the weather before venturing out into the waters.*" These profound words made sense to the Shompen boy and he nodded.

Then the two made a key decision. Nothing short of a conspiracy in their communities. Something to break free of the shackles of the closeknit bonding. How did that thought process germinate? No one may actually know as the boys had probably greater exposure to the outside world than many of their peers. Kayat's visit to the town had probably infused in him a desire to explore. The school lessons had only invigorated those feelings. He was the one who initiated by saying, "*lets try to understand the lifestyle of the other indigenous people. It would be interesting to look at how they have lived in the other forests. It would give us a better perspective of the struggles and challenges that they face.*" Tibo was initially reluctant but then he too was not bereft of the adventure genes. He seemed to be sucked into the thought process of his friend. He literally caved in and agreed to the proposal. The conspiracy had been finally hatched.

****

CHAPTER VII

Pilot Run

The difficult part of the conspiracy was the plan of action. The two boys thought over for some time. They tried to recollect what was taught to them in school. It was Tibo who first alluded to the Jarawas. From what was told to them, they seemed adept at both the forest dwelling as well as catching fish in the waters. Very much akin to the lifestyle of the Nicobarese thought the latter primarily dwelt on the coasts. The Shompen boy too let his thoughts wander. He looked at the geography of the islands from one of the maps which he had taken from a school book. Getting to the Andamans was the best way to explore all the tribes in the region. Hence, he agreed to the proposal.

The modus operandi for their plan was the next step. The boys had no clue on this and decided to look at this later. Probably ask the teacher about this. But then there was the fear of their plan spilling out. It was to be done in the most innocuous way. So they decided to return to their villages and plan out later. After all, the distances were large and it was not just about using the Nicobarese canoe to sail to such far distances. The return was difficult since the two boys were still not completely familiar with the routes. However, they used their navigational skills well and returned. The elders questioned them on the absence but were not suspicious since the boys had brought back some fruits with them.

The next session in school was a week away. The boys were not sure if both of them would be allowed to go there. But luck was in their favour as there were no specific chores which the boys were asked to stay back were. It was a different group of the two tribes with a strength of around 15. It was a challenge since many were new and were more stunned by the surroundings. It took them some time to get to terms and even sit on the chairs. The boys used this time to talk up about their plans. The focus was on how to elicit information. It was not going to be an easy task without arousing any suspicion.

The class began and the teacher once again focussed on the tribes of the region. For the two, this was a repetition but for the new ones, it was something different and astounding. Kayat saw this as an opportunity and asked the teacher, "*Do these different tribes ever meet?*" The teacher responded in the negative. Tibo then came to the point and asked about how people travelled from one island to the other. The teacher took it as a sign of curiosity and simply mentioned that there were ferries that went from one island to the other. He himself had been to Andamans and visited the other tribes. There was no sign of any suspicion. Instead, he was happy that the two were curious. No one else in the class seemed to ask anything. Even the elders who had accompanied the boys were curious about what these ferries were. The teacher showed them some photographs and all of them were shocked. It looked like supersized boats with a number of windows. Moreover, it carried a lot of people and looked more advanced than the canoes. The boys understood that without such large vessels, they would not be able to traverse the long distances. The situation seemed a bit hopeless for them.

While the boys were tense, they still went through the classes. The teacher was also focussed on them since they seemed to be the brightest and more inquisitive. Those relating to the flora and fauna of the region was almost on their fingertips. The Shompen boy wondered that he could have also taken the classes since he was not fairly conversant with both the languages. It was as if the elder and teacher had read his mind. He was called to the front to talk about his settlement. It was a surprise for him since he had never addressed a group. There was that initial diffidence but he gathered his thoughts. Tibo was also supportive of his friend and that calmed his nerves. The other students were giggling as they had not seen a peer of their age address them. There was a strict hierarchy in the communities they came from and it was only the elders who could address or advise them. This was a new element in the mix.

Kayat moved forward and stood in front of the class. He began with a light banter welcoming the students in their language. This broke the ice and even the teacher was impressed. He then began talking about his community and himself. It was interesting to the Shompen boys who lived a similar life. However, the few Nicobarese boys who were in school and who still stayed in the forests did not understand him. After that first address, he switched to the other language. The elders and the teacher were stunned. Here was a boy who knew the other language despite no formal schooling. The words were broken and it was accentuated but the general import of the words was clear. The Nicobarese laughed at the accent but then they too were surprised at the boy speaking their tongue.

With the passage of time, he oozed confidence. The voice became louder and the teacher too was impressed at his vocal abilities. After a general overview of his community, he began narrating interesting anecdotes. The other boys were glued onto what he said. It seemed something coming out the local boy seemed more authentic that what was being parroted by their teacher. It was like a person living the grassroots life narrating everyday life and its struggles. He somehow had the knack of keeping the audience engaged. After a few narrations, he wanted the class to also join in and talk about similar instances. Things like catching a pig, plucking fruits, climbing trees, running after monkeys, laying the bait for fishing, playing etc. The other boys were diffident initially but then joined in as they could relate to their own lives.

The teacher was truly impressed despite not understanding fully what the kids spoke. The elders also joined in. For them it was a new experience trying to relate their own way of life. While they had spoken to the administration about some of this, it was always a guarded approach. Here, these boys were engaging in a no holds barred conversation and seemed to be relishing it. Normally, the conversations back in the community were limited and business like since a hierarchy was followed. However, the situation here seemed quite different as the children were in a way expressing themselves. However, having grown up in a strict regimen, they nursed a sense of skepticism too.

The class went on and everyone lost count of time. They passed the lunch break as the engagement level was very high. The teacher also did not interrupt since he found that this was a good means of learning for all. While the content was the same, it was the methodology that seemed to have worked wonders. The topics vacillated to many aspects, all fulcrumed around life in the islands and the community. Some narrated their experiences, the good, bad and ugly ones. After all, life in these pristine parts were a paradox of what nature itself was, the uncertainty of beauty and the beast. Basically, one could not take anything for granted and had to respect it.

The boy invited his friend Tibo to also come in front. There was that inhibition, not surprising for a boy who had little exposure to all this. However, the presence of Kayat changed all that and he shed that diffidence to come forward. He deviated a bit and talked about the road that had come up near his community. Some of the other boys were aware of it but had not breached the topic. He first spoke about how vehicles had started plying on it. The speed, sound and the ability to transport people were talked about. After all it was like an advanced toy for the kids who used local materials for making these playthings. He then spoke about how some outsiders gave them food to eat like biscuits. "*It is tasty no doubt*", he said but "*it is not good for us*". The teacher was surprised at this statement since everyone scrambled to get these eatables from outsiders. The maturity of the boy was beyond his years and this statement exemplified it. The class however did not agree with him since they eagerly awaited for these goodies. The discussion then went around whether the road itself was good for them. One of the boys stood up and said, "*they cut down a number of trees to make that road*". Some others said that it made them reach their destinations faster. Others chipped in saying that the bridge over the stream had led to a lot of waste being thrown on the banks by outsiders. The ecological aspect of development was something ingrained in them.

After the lunch break, the class dispersed. The food was sumptuous made of pandunus fruit and rice. The children were also given some juice which they relished. It was important for their long journey ahead. The boys decided to stay together until their paths took different turns for the settlement. They sat for some time on the ground taking stock of the situation. The Shompen boy broke the silence stating, "*we need to find a ferry*". "*But who will give us a ride on it and even if someone did, they would all be suspicious,*" replied Tibo. They thought for some time and the situation did not seem very optimistic. Kayat then said, "*maybe we do not need to go all the way to the Andamans. We can take a canoe and hop from one island to the other in the Nicobar. When we reach the top most island, we can then look at a larger vessel to take us.*" He seemed to have a good idea of the geography of the islands with the map fully ingrained in him. Tibo thought for some time on this idea and remembered an elder of his settlement who had gone to one of the nearer islands on his canoe. "*I will ask for his help.*" The boy was skeptical of this idea but then the two had nothing better. So it was decided that this option would be tried and if the man grew suspicious, then the plan was going down the drain. Then all of a sudden, the boy grew confident enough to say, "*Let us try to row ourselves and try to cross the island.*" Tibo looked at his friend in amusement. "*I can barely row and you have no experience. We won't be able to make it even to the next island.*" Kayat was however confident. "*We will practise and then only venture into the deep waters. After all both of us are good swimmers and should be able to navigate any disasters.*" Tibo was nevertheless hesitant. "*Swimming in the rivers, ponds and close to the sea are very different from that in the deep waters. It is not going to be an easy task. And then I have this bouts of fever. The burden then would be on you."*

Youthful exuberance had however overtaken all these inhibitions. The two had decided to take the perilous journey in whatever canoe they could muster. Tibo then remembered about an abandoned canoe on the shores. It was not far from where they were and hence they trudged to the place. It was exactly in the place where the Nicobarese boy had mentioned. It was a large one made of local wood and fibres. But there were some gaping holes. Tibo then recounted, "*This was once used to go to a far off island north of this place. However, its owner who had left it at the very spot met with an unfortunate death due to a fall from a tree. His family did not want to do fishing and instead concentrated on hunting and food gathering. The community elders wanted to dismantle it for making some new huts but the memory of that man prevented them from taking this to a logical end. Hence, the structure remained abandoned.*" It was as if destined to be used for that long journey. Both of them quickly made an assessment of the repairs to be done. There were oars too on the canoe. Finally, the boys worked out what was needed and decided to come there later. They did not want to be delayed and arouse suspicion of the elders. It was for this very purpose and they decided not to seek help of anyone for the repair of the canoe too.

With all the bubbly enthusiasm, they made their way back to the settlement. For youngsters, it was like a project that they were undertaking but one which required a lot of stealth and patience. No one outside the close family should have an inkling of all his in the community or else it may blow up. They would only tell their parents that they were going on a project around the island and would return in a few days. Suspicion would have been aroused but yet it had to be done.

In a couple of days, the rendezvous happened at the beachhead where the canoe was there. Both of them brought some materials to repair the vessel. It took a long time since both were new to this field. Tibo in one of the fishing expeditions, the day before, had studied some of the other canoes of his community. However, he did not want to arouse the suspicion of the elders and was quite subtle about it. He was also involved in the construction of some of these canoes and had a good idea about it. However, he needed the Shompen boy to boost his confidence. The latter despite his lack of experience, was not in awe of what they would finally have. An hour of good labour got the vessel back to a semblance of something sturdy. But would it be able to navigate if the waters were choppy. Only time would tell the reality.

They carried the vessel to the open waters. Everything seemed fine as it hit the shallow waters of the wide seas. The two decided to test it as they went along the coastline. It responded well and withstood the test of some waves that hit the shores. Kayat was a bit taken aback at the rocking of the vessel. It was clear that it was his first time and he was not sure of his moorings. But a child brought up in the lap of nature got back his gumption without showing any signs of fear. For him the waters were like the rivers and streams on which he swam. Little did he know about its salinity which resulted in a different breed of fish and other marine creatures that traversed it. The boys went along the shoreline for some time. They did venture into the deeper waters too before returning to the shallow ones. With time, they gained confidence and experimented with some zig zag moves too. It was all about understanding the limits to which they could test the vessel. But the Shompen boy was well aware of the need to respect nature which could be unforgiving. His life in the dense woods had taught him this basic tenet of life. Tibo was cautious since he had seen some canoe topple with fatal results. The sea was more unforgiving than the rivers and streams, not only in terms of depth but the uncertainty in the turbulence of its waters. Moreover, it was also vulnerable to attacks by predatory fishes like the reef sharks that were all over the waters of the island.

The time for experimentation was over and Tibo decided to tether the canoe onto the shores. It was quite a distance from where they had entered the sea but he knew that this was the direction that they needed to go for hitting the nearest island. He had gone once in a similar canoe with some elders and was aware of the general direction. However, he was just in the dark about any other islands. All the geography taught to him in the class seems theoretical to him beyond that one island. However, with the general direction, the two boys hoped to go beyond what their elders had done. Possibly even touching the Andamans. Something that no one would have imagined was possible by two youngsters with limited experience of the seas. They seemed well prepared and ready to fight another day. So with the confidence level, they decided to embark on their journey in a couple of days. In the meantime, they stocked the canoe with fruits and nuts for the perilous adventure ahead.

****

CHAPTER VIII

Journey to the Andamans

So the D-day arrived. Both the boys had a fidgety night. What lay ahead? Would they be able to return alive? What was the purpose of all this risk taking when they were living their comfortable lives? Would their brethren in other islands turn hostile? Would the Sentinelese spare them? All thoughts running in a hurry. But nothing out of the ordinary since they were embarking upon an adventure which none of their ilk ever had. Anyhow it was planned to meet early in the morning before others in the community got up. Both of them had already told their parents that they would be away in the island and would return in a few days. There was no hint of any suspicion since it was normal for people to get lost in the woods and return later. Moreover, the boys were sturdy enough to take of themselves in case of any eventuality or attack from animals.

Both of them managed to slip out stealthily from their settlements. The parents or siblings were in deep sleep, too tired from the previous day's exertion. It took some time for both of them to reach the spot where the canoe was located. The woods were dense and they had to make do with general directions and the position of the sun. The Shompen boy reached earlier as his plan was to hit the shores and then walk along it. On the other hand, Tibo took a detour which had to be corrected but he too managed to hit the beachhead and then went along the rocky shores. He was feeling much better this morning despite a bout of fever in the night. -By the time they met, the sun had already come out and it was warm. It was a paradox for the two, happy to see each other but tension filled the air. It was a journey that was beset with a lot of uncertainties including the possibility of being fatal. Despite the butterflies in the stomach, it was clear that there was no going back. The sense of bravado had not diminished and they would follow where fate would take them.

So firstly, they took stock of the supplies on the canoe. Apart from what was already stocked, they had collected some other fruits too. However, it was pointless loading the canoe too much since weight could make it unstable. Hence, they had to have the right balance. Moreover, these were boys who could survive for long periods without food if the circumstances so demanded. Thus, they were all ready to embark on their journey.

It was one push and they both jumped in. The imbalance in the weight almost toppled the canoe to one side but the Shompen boy managed to correct the tilt. It would have been one comical start to the journey. They vessel then pushed into deeper waters as the two began to row it. Despite the initial hiccup, the two were full of enthusiasm ready to start their tryst. Tibo told his friend to relax since it would be a long journey and they needed to conserve energy. First, they went along the shore and at a particular point, the Nicobarese boy said that they now needed to head in the direction of the deep sea to reach another island. His friend put energy into his strokes as the canoe headed into deeper water. The sea was calmer here and very soon the views of the land faded. They were now in the middle of the deep waters. Kayat queried Tibo on whether they were going in the right direction. The latter nodded stating that "*this is how I went on the last journey to the nearest island*". They kept quiet and started rowing. With no land in the horizon, a tinge of fear crept into the two boys. They were now on their own and it was hope that they were going in the right direction.

Silence engulfed and the boys kept on their efforts. It was an eerie feeling as the only sound that came was of the lapping of the waves as the oars hit the water. Not a single bird was visible and it seemed as if the canoe and its passengers were all alone. The boys did see some fishes but the concentration on their task was so immense that it all seemed to fade into oblivion. It was a good hour of this absolute quiet before Tibo uttered the word, "*we are making good progress. The speed is faster than when I went last time.*" This was a piece of motivation for his friend who suddenly was infused with chunks of motivation. The rowing became faster and the boy also started to relax a bit watching the marine creatures move below the surface of the water. Tibo started feeling weak during this phase and he felt his body getting hot. So he restrained his efforts.

It was then that the two realised that there was no need to have that silence and they could relax. This might actually calm the nerves without affecting their performance. The realisation was spontaneous and Kayat then talked about the school. "*What a lovely place it was with all those friends. We used to get good food to eat and the teachers taught us so much about our culture and values. There is such a vast world out there and we are not aware of all this.*" Tibo then talked about the fun that they had playing. "*Remember that game we played with those strange rules. It was so entertaining.*" The Shompen boy agreed. The two then began talking about their life and how they became friends. The culture of the two tribes was also the point of discussion. Amidst all this talk, they forgot about time. Suddenly, the Nicobarese boy shouted, "*Do you see the land over there*". Kayat could see some lines in the distance. "*Yes, we have reached an island,*", he shouted in joy. The sun was beating down but the joy was so immense that the two forgot about the heat. It was great to see them conquering the first hurdle. This may have been their most important one too since hopping from one island to the next had given them the confidence of reaching others too.

As they rowed faster, the silhouette of the land came closer. They could not make out the treelines in the distance. Yet the distance was far and it took them atleast half an hour before they could make out clearly the contours of the beachhead. Tibo then changed the direction of the canoe to make to move away from the edges to somewhere towards the centre of the island. "*We landed in the place where we are going now. It has a larger beach and we can rest for some time*", he said. So it took the boys some time before they could reach the intended destination. It was a sense of immense accomplishment as they touched land. The strange part was that they had not consumed a single fruit stocked on deck despite the long journey. It was a picture of immense concentration that made the two forget about what they had on board. It was only when they got into the land that they felt pangs of hunger and thirst. It was time to rest and consume some of this stock that they had got. Before that they had to hide the canoe so that no one could find it. They chose a dense part of the woods to keep the vessel. It was not easy since the boys were tired and had to carry the canoe. The two enjoyed the edibles that they brought with them. However, when the Shompen boy took a scoop of water, he understood that it was saline and spat it out. His friend laughed.

The two were too tired to explore the island they landed. They simply slumped and slept off. When they woke, both felt thirsty. But they could not consume the sea water and had to search. They decided to go into the woods. It was not very different from their island and in some parts was even less dense. The familiarity of the surroundings enabled them to make good progress. Soon, they reached a stream and began gulping down the fresh water. It was so refreshing. Suddenly a group of monkeys came over to quench their thirst. They looked at the boys with surprise and kept staring. This was perplexing to the two since they were used to these creatures running away in fear of being hunted. Their hypothesis was that there was no human being on the island and hence the monkeys did not have that fear.

However, little did the boys know that they were on Little Nicobar which is also inhabited. They took their gaze off them and began drinking the water. The animals remained curious but did not try to confront the two. There was no standoff, so as to say. Each quenching their thirst.

The boys then came back to the place where the canoe was berthed. No sooner were they resting that a group of tribal elders came up. They seemed to be on a fishing expedition and had some spears with them. The boys were taken aback but they had no defence. They spoke in Nicobarese and asked them about their mission. They looked like the men of the forests, not the ones who had integrated with mainstream society.The two had planned well and told the men that they lived on the other side of the island and had lost the way. It was a surprise to the elders who did not expect two boys to be able to traverse a long distance. Nevertheless, the woods were thick and it was surprising that some youngsters lost their way. The discussed among themselves but did not seem to adopting any adversial stance. They seemed more focussed on their own task and went their own way. Fortunately for the boys, they did not see the canoe. It had been well hidden in the undergrowth. The tribesmen then told the boys to go in a particular direction and left them. It was a sigh of relief for the two since it could have spilled the beans.

After the men left, the boys took stock of the situation and decided their next course of action. They had rested well and now had to think about what to do. There was enough stock of food. There was no need to take any extra load of goodies. A decision was to be made if they should start off immediately or wait till the break of dawn the next day. The boys were not sure of the time taken until their encounter with the next island. By the distances shown on the map in school, it seemed longer than the journey they had just undertaken. Hence, they would require the requisite rest before this next phase. Prudence took over the element of bravado and the boys decided to rest.

The canoe hidden in the woods was a good base for their temporary settlement. It was covered with some leaves which acted as a bed. Now they were ready to explore the island a bit before resting. It was still not dusk but the two were quite tired after the strain of rowing. The Shompen boy seemed more exhausted as he had in the enthusiasm expended more energy. Tibo with the experience of rowing had conserved himself better. Nevertheless, they did not want to sleep off so early when there was adequate light. The two thus made their way into the woods eager to see the flora and fauna of the island.

It was a slow trudge as the woods became thick. It didn't seem that any humans had made their way through the path they were taken. Anyhow, this seemed a good omen as they would not encounter any other tribesmen. The more number of people knew of their presence, the more difficult it would be for them. It was important not to arouse any curiosity. Moreover, it was not clear if the other men they encountered would come back to see if the boys were still there. It could spoil all their well orchestrated plans to explore the archipelago. The boys came across a snake which scurried off into the woods. There were more varieties of birds on the island and they were making a cacophony. Especially the parakeets. Probably after noticing the boys who had intruded into their pristine environment. Kayat told his friend that the sounds were a warning to the other animals. He had studied the nature of birds back around his home. This was an area of interest for him and he would spend hours studying them.

Finally, the boys reached a stream. A small one but the flow of water was fairly brisk. The boys noticed that there were some small crabs and fish. A frog too jumped on the sight of the boy and scooted to the interiors. The two washed their hands and feet in the cold waters of the stream. They poured some on their faces to refresh themselves. It was a tiring day and they needed every ounce of energy for the days ahead. They sat at the banks of the stream for some time. It was an elixir. The boys chatted about the school days and their new found friendship. With the passage of time, this was about reinforcing the fact that their journey was a useful one seeking to understand the other cultures. There were moments when they felt as to whether this was worth all this effort. Especially, thinking about the stories of the Sentinelese who were known to have killed many outsiders. These moments were interspersed with a myriad of emotions from optimism to despair. But somehow it all came down to both being convinced that the journey was worth all the effort.

It was time to go back to their temporary home, the canoe. Tibo then suggested that they could catch some fish from the stream. Both the boys then made some ramshackle tools and tried to spear some. It was a comical effort since they did not have the usual fishing tackle. Finally, they managed to catch a few. It was a mixture of patience and perseverance. They put the catch in some arecanut leaves which were lying on the ground. It was neatly wrapped up for being carried back to the canoe.

They briefly got lost on the way but managed to hit the shore. The journey along the rocky beaches got them to the point where they had disembarked on the island. From there the walk to the deep woods was easier. They reached the place before dusk, a good timing indeed. Then it was time to infuse some energy with some fruits that they had carried. The boys took the fish from the leaves. They were cleaned and the scales removed with the implements they had. For lighting up a fire, they used some stones. It was something they had learnt well from the life in the forest. They then heated it up over a slow fire like a barbeque. There were no vessels. They kept a watch to see if it was well cooked. When the body became brownish they removed it. They each took a bite off it. It did not taste as well without the other ingredients. But nevertheless, it was palatable. Both the boys were used to having such food when they ventured away from their settlements. The Shompen boy liked it since it was a freshwater one while Tibo preferred the sea fish which tasted differently. They ate to their hearts full. Then it was time for the fruits which they relished. It was washed down with some water which they had collected.

After having energised themselves, it was now time to take stock of the plan ahead. Both thought for some time and then ideated. It was a free flow of thoughts ranging from visiting the indigenous people on this island to resting to leaving the island on the break of dawn without wasting any time. On the first option, the two already met some fishermen who did not seem very different from their own looks and possibly their lifestyles too. Hence, given the risk of meeting them and not learning anything significant, they dropped the idea. The second option would only waste more time in their endeavour. So with all the bravado, they decided to venture out into the seas as soon as possible. They had already made an image of the next island from the piece of paper that Kayat had. It was much further than this one. They had rested enough and were energised to take on this journey.

The first part was to get to the northern part of Little Nicobar. From this point onwards, there were some islands which would be stop over points before venturing into the next big island. They would need to get around the shores and reach the northern tip. Quite akin to what they had done in the case of the Great Nicobar. However, this island was smaller than theirs and would take lesser time. It was not easy to gauge without the instruments for direction. Both the boys had made a good study of the map of the island and were aware of some rocky outcrops there. However, seeing first and exploring based on some secondary information were something else.

Without wasting any time, they boarded the canoe and started rowing close to the shores. After sometime, they saw some indigenous men who were on the shores. They raised some sound and the boys could barely make out what they said. It didn't seem prudent to come ashore as the tenor of their call was not overtly friendly. They were fishermen who had their own canoe and seemed to be threatening to come onto the waters. The boys hid under some leaves on board and started rowing stealthily. It was a tense standoff and the boys could just hope that they did not come after them. The men on the shore were a bit confused. They probably assumed that these boys were from some other settlement on the island. Moreover, since they were rowing away from them, there did not seem to be any threat. So whatever went through their minds, they were not keen to follow and confront them. This was a sigh of relief. The Shompen boy spoke first, "*That was a close shave. Now they will inform their elders.*" "*Don't worry*", said Tibo. "*They might just assume it was boys from the other settlements out for fishing. It is just that they don't want anyone to come into their waters. We are anyway away from them.*"

The boys waited for some time before removing the leaves from their body. They could then row as fast as possible away from the sight of the men. In this melee, they were not sure if they had reached the northern tip of the island. Both of them studied the topography and decided that they would need to move a bit further before the rocky outcrops loomed in the distance. They were pleased to see it and were sure that they had reached the rendezvous point. From here, it was a journey up north before they hit some of the small islands. These would be stopovers before the next large one. If they had to reach the large island before dusk, there was no way they could try to rest in the northern tipoff this island. So the two decided to give it a test without coming ashore. There was just a few moments to regroup. After all they had expended a lot of energy while rowing away from the men on the shore. The short rest was enough for the two to get going. It was a close shave and now they were on their own again.

CHAPTER IX

The Hopover Islands

They headed out into the open seas. They were just hoping that the direction was correct. It was a long haul as the waters seemed choppy. They had to use the flow of the waves to sail along. Rowing itself was giving much leverage. Slowly the land behind them nearly disappeared in the horizon. However, there were no silhouettes visible ahead. They were in the open waters. The boys decided not to let the situation overwhelm them as they kept rowing. Every five minutes or so, they looked up to see it land was visible. Then suddenly, it was eureka moment as the Shompen boy scanned the horizon and saw some treelines on his left. "*Look there*", he shouted. There were indeed traces of land. The canoe was going in the wrong direction. They corrected that and rowed towards land. It took them good time to reach the island. Getting the canoe onshore was the most difficult part since they needed to drag it along the sandy shores. With all the strain, it was time to take a well earned rest.

After sitting on the sands and washing themselves in the cool waters, it was time to look around. The island had some forests but these were not as dense as back home. One could make out the entire landscape of the land and it definitely seemed smaller. There were some undulating hillocks up front but not very high. They decided to see what could be collected. There were some fruits and berries on the trees. A stream flowed along the land with fresh water. The boys lapped it up. After all they were tired and thirsty. They ate some fruits and brought back some with them. After the much needed rest, it was time for the next part of the journey.

With the general directions of north, they embarked on the next leg of their journey. The waters had calmed down and it was a long way ahead. With experience, they kept a track of the island that they were leaving so as not to be taken off track. They also co-ordinated the rowing well with both taking turns to keep a watch. After the silhouette of the island had disappeared from the horizon, they noticed a big vessel some distance away. It looked like the large ship which the teacher had shown them. Prudence demanded that they keep away from the path of that ship. So they rowed in the opposite direction with the attendant danger of being away from their intended path. The sign of a large vessel was also an indication that they were close to shore.

With the detour, the distance seemed much larger as they kept up the efforts. With the experience gained, it was better conservation of human effort coupled with a lookout for any vessels or land. The Shompen boy was getting accustomed to the open sea and began to lose any fear of being in such waters with nothing in sight. For someone who had lived all his life in the dense forests with no experience of the sea, it was a remarkable transition to this new way of life. The waters hitting against the canoe were actually a calming influence on him. It seemed to convey a hidden message that they were on the right track. With the large vessel also vanishing in the distance, the boys changed track to their original one. And lo behold, a treeline loomed up in the distance. It was still far and they had to make their way with some effort to touch on the beachhead. This one also seemed quite small compared to the previous one. While coming closer, they could identify some canoes in the distance. It was clear that this was an inhabited island and they wanted to avoid it.

No sooner had they touched based and taken the canoe to a hiding place that a group of five men came out of the bushes with their hunting tools. There was no way out and the boys had to give in. They were too tired to even attempt an escape. They were Nicobarese tribes quite similar in appearance to Tibo except that they had proper clothes on. Looked like they were those who had integrated with mainstream society, as the cousins of Tibo were. They were however, more curious on Kayat and asked him on the place from where he had come. It was obvious that they had not seen a Shompen. Tibo had a pre-decided story that he was from another island and gone out fishing into the deep waters. Kayak was his friend of another family staying in the same island. Choppy waters had led them astray and they were stranded now. A couple of men did not believe the story trying to ask them about the family members. The boys did not distort the names or numbers of their family members back home.

Now the focus was on the Shompen boy. He looked very different and the men had not seen anyone like that? How could he be on the same island? Nevertheless, the boys were in luck as the men took some sympathy at the two youngsters for a perilous journey just for making the ends meet for their families. One of them offered to come along with them to the island which the boys could not blatantly refuse. However, the Shompen boy stepped in and said that they were confident of getting back to their island now but would appreciate if some edibles could be given. The men gave a part of their catch. They then left without much ado. After all they may have also had to reach their destinations in time. It was a close shave but an important aspect in the lives of the indigenous people. Unless threatened, you don't poke your nose into each other's life. It is a matter of respecting each other.

Finally, the two boys stocked their canoes with the edibles given. It was now time for them to rest. It was a hot afternoon and the sun was beating down. While they were refreshed, the urge to explore further seemed limited. It was as if the body was not willing to look at another journey. However, the Shompen boy had a gut feeling that once the men who they encountered went back to their settlement, there was a possibility of a change in mood. He somehow felt uncomfortable especially since his features were different from the Andamanese which was a source of suspicion. His gut feel was well founded. No sooner than the boys had packed their canoe and had entered the waters did some men emerge out of the bushes and were running into the water. They shouted and then threw some pebbles at the boys. They did not want to pursue them since the boys had a headstart. However, they were surprised that the boys were headed in the direction opposite to which they had come.

The two did not look back. They wanted to hit the deep waters as soon as possible. It was only after a good fifteen minutes that the boys stopped and took a deep breath. They were tired after the efforts and the shoreline was also moving out of their view. They took stock of the situation and believed that they had deviated from their path. They had to push a bit west to the nearest island. They corrected the path and were now in open waters. The afternoon sun was severe and they did not much time to think about it. Time was not on their side and they did not want to be stuck in the waters at dusk. So the eagerness and anxiety made them dissipate a lot of energy as they stretched every bit of their sinew in the quest to get land. What they did not know was that the next big island, the Katchall was a good distance and could even take them an entire day to traverse. They had to cross the Sombrero channel that separated the two islands. Nevertheless, they kept the pace in the hope of reaching their destination fast.

However, as the afternoon passed, the sun was in the phase of setting. The boys still did not see any land ahead and were wondering if they had taken the right direction. They did not want to be disheartened and kept up the effort. Fortunately, the sea was calm and they could hear the lapping of their oars on the quiet water surface. There were a flock of birds that flew overhead. It was a sign that land was not far and this pumped them up. They rested for a while to refresh themselves with fruits and some berries. There was no fresh water on board and neither wanted to use the sea water for sustenance. They could see some fishes skimming the surface but made no effort to catch it. After all, they were focussed on their goal of reaching the large island.

However, despite all the efforts, land was nowhere to be seen. It was slowly getting dark and anxiety crept up. The boys were left wondering if they had taken the right direction. The entire horizon was scanned but with fading light, the visibility was also poor. They could see the sun set over the horizon. Rather than admiring the beauty of the ball of fire going over the water, they were praying to buy more daylight. That was of course not going to happen. With the sun having set, it became dark the waters now had an eerie feeling. Both the boys had not experienced such a situation. Sitting on the rocky shores and admiring the sea at night was a different proposition. Here it was in the middle of the waters, albeit not very choppy. It was a clear night too and the light of the moon and stars did light up the place. But it was little comfort.

Slowly, the boys with all the will power gathered from the experience in the woods, began to feel a bit more comforted. It was clear to them that this was a long haul. Even with all this light, it would be difficult to spot any land. The hours went by and slowly the two got accustomed to the environment around them. There were moments when they heard some splashes in the water. Probably some fishes skimming the water. Maybe a large marine creature that signalled danger. But the two did not flinch. They had to ride out this rough patch. Kayat was the first to speak, "*I am sure we are headed in the right direction. Even if it gets late, we will reach the big island.*" That was reassuring for his friend. After all, both of them were in together and had to collectively take on the challenge. The canoe wafted stealthily over the calm waters. The two could however feel the oars hitting the liquid mass. It gave them a false sense of moving fast.

They took turns to row as the vessel moved ahead into nothingness. Each of them kept the other motivated. There were phases of silence. Time however passed but the boys continued with their efforts. When one put in the strain, the other rested and refreshed themselves with some edibles. It was a co-ordinated effort. And they were beginning to enjoy it despite all the uncertainty. It was important that they did not fall asleep. Soon the night seemed to be passing by and there were signs that dawn would crack. Or was it wishful thinking of the two? The silence was broken by a feeble cry from the Shompen boy, "*light, light*", he said. Tibo looked in that direction and yes, they could make out some faint light in the distance.

They began rowing in that direction. Just then, an element of fear crept in as to whether it was a large vessel. That would mean that they had not found land yet with a greater risk of them being out in the open sea. With utmost caution and a sense of purpose, they bridged the gap between the light and themselves as the illumination seemed to get brighter and larger. The sky was also getting a bit lighted with signs of dawn. They had hit a double whammy which looked too good to be true. As they approached towards the light, the boys picked up the silhouette of trees. It was indeed an island and a eureka moment for them. They let out a scream of joy. They had covered a humongous distance rowing all through the night. It was a test of their mettle and will power and they had come out trump.

The island indeed looked large. However, as they neared closer to the shore, they saw some small structures. The Shompen boy immediately recognised the ones he saw in the town back home. They were settlements of outsiders. He immediately signalled to his friend to move away from that. If they were sighted, their entire plan may come to nought. So they moved further away from the light. They could see another canoe near the shore. Probably the fishermen were trying for a catch in the early hours of the day. They too spotted the boys and seemed curious. However, they were busy with their own errands and did not try to come close to the boy's canoe. So the boys were in luck.

They moved their canoe onto a pristine part of the shore. Away from the settlement with a peaceful place to rest. When they hit the shore, they did not even attempt to hide the canoe. Both were thoroughly exhausted and wanted to just rest on the shores. It was an achievement of sorts for them. All alone in the high seas and managing to reach the large island. Even though the journey was still a long way over, they had set a benchmark and zipped up their confidence levels. They finished off whatever refreshments that were on the canoe. After the well earned rest, they would need to stock more for the next journey. But before that a nap was the order of the day.

The boys woke only after a few hours. They were sleep deprived and had to make up for it. It was now time to search for a stream. They moved into the woods and after a brisk walk managed to find one. It was time to wash themselves and drink to heart content. The woods were thick and they could find the fruits and other edibles needed to stock their canoe.

Then they retraced back to the shore and the canoe. They decided to take the canoe to the northern most point of the island for the next leg of the journey. They would then rest there and stock the vessel before embarking on the journey the next day morning.

With the aching legs and arms, it took them some time to muster the energy to move the canoe out in to the waters. They rowed along the shores and reached a vantage point. The next island was not as far as this one, atleast in the maps. However, they needed to move in the right direction for that. This time, they managed to hide their canoe in the wild growth and went in search of fruits. These woods had a better stock of edibles than the previous point. They managed to stock the canoe. It was getting late and the boys rested on their vessel. With all the energy drained from their nighttime tryst, they fell asleep. Not even the night insects could trouble them and they woke up only with the crack of dawn. It was time for the next leg of their journey.

With confidence oozing, they then set out for the next island, Teressa. It was going to be a relatively shorter one but the concern was only about the direction. They could see some fishing vessels in the distance but wanted to avoid those. The tell tale signs of the strain of the previous days were not visible and it seemed that they had recovered well. Slowly but surely, the island they started off from was fading from visibility. This was a sign that both of them made good progress. They took a last glimpse behind and there was nothing to make out. They were now in the open waters. After a couple of hours of brisk rowing, they sighed something ahead. After progressing, it was clear that this was a small island. The two were not overtly excited since this was not their destination for rest. Given the situation, they decided not to touch base here. The confidence level was high enough for them to bypass this and move further up.

They circled around the island and entered open waters again. They wanted to reach the large island well in time. Clouds started developing overhead and this was not a good sign. If it rained, then the situation would be difficult. Fortunately, the clouds just shielded them from the heat of the sun. They were not big enough to cause a downpour. It helped them move faster towards their destination. It was phases of rest for one of them to recoup while the other put in all the effort. They had developed a sort of rhythm in their rowing as the vessel steadily moved forward. The two lost count of time with the focus on seeing the clouds above and signs of any land. They even saw some land far away but could gauge that this too was a small outcrop from the sea. They bypassed that too and went about in the direction which they believed was correct.

As the afternoon progressed, the clouds were playing cat and mouse. However, it did not develop into the heavy ones that would cause a shower. The ocean no longer scared these boys as they were focussed on their objective. The Shompen boy was surprised at the level of comfort that he had developed towards the open waters. Something about which he had very little inkling of in life before embarking on this journey. The adventure bug had bitten deep into him and his friend. They were enjoying it despite knowing about the perils that nature could spring up. Finally, it was dusk and the same dark surroundings. This time, there was no moonlight and stars to show them the way. The dark clouds had shielded everything. It was again threatening to rain. This time the threat was for real as a downpour started. It was probably the worst time for that since it completely masked the little visibility. It was for the first time that the two had been exposed to such a weather in the high seas. Even the most hardy fishermen could be shaken in such circumstances. But the two held onto their nerves. One of them was on the lookout while the other person rowed. The visibility was nearly zero as water splashed on the canoe. It rained for sometime and they had to remove the water from the canoe on a regular basis. The going was definitely tough but then the weather gods became kinder.

The rains stopped and water had been removed from the canoe. However, there was still no signs of light ahead. As usual, the two took turns to row. Then suddenly out of the blue, they could make out some lights on the right. If it was the same island, then they were going astray into deeper waters. So they took stock of the situation and started rowing towards the direction of the light. It was a providential escape since it they hadn't seen the flicker of light, they may have gone into deeper waters. But luck had been kind to them.

As they neared the shores, it was evident that the light would be from some structure made by the outsiders. It was time to be cautious and select a desolate place to touch ashore. They talked for some time and then decided to go ahead of that light. They could make out some mangrove plantations adjoining the water. This was not a good place to berth. They moved ahead to search for open land. Up ahead, they could make out a rocky beach that seemed good enough. It was difficult to bring the boat aboard in the dark. The sky was a bit clearer and some stars helped them out. It was still not easy as the two dragged the canoe into the bushes. They ate the stock on board and slumped into the canoe for a nap.

The exhaustion was evident as they went into a deep slumber. The two woke up only to the cacophony of some monkeys who spotted them. The sun had light up the day and it was strange that the two could only arise now. This was unusual for their way of life when they slept early and woke up early too at the crack of dawn. The adventure had disrupted their biological cycle with the element of uncertainty thrown in the mixture. The monkeys were only curious and scooted away as soon as the two woke up. They stretched themselves ready to take stock of what to do. The first thing was to find water. With the type of experience they had in the woods, it was easy and soon they found a stream. To wash themselves and quench their thirst. It was only with all this that they had really woken up and come to their senses. They had finally reached the large island and had traversed more than halfway of the Nicobar group of islands.

This was their toughest journey since they had weathered a downpour and a storm. It was a test of their resolve and they had come with flying colours. As Gregory Williams had quoted, "*On the other side of a storm is the strength that comes from having navigated through it.*" They had indeed garnered that strength for the rest of their journey.

****

****

CHAPTER X

Last Leg to Car Nicobar

The real test of crossing to the Car Nicobar island awaited them. It was not an easy one since the distance was much longer. A decision had to be made if they could cross it with this canoe or seek help. A direct rowing from the northern tip of this island could take even two days and nights. It was something which seemed a difficult proposition. Moreover, it was not necessary that the sea would be as calm as they found in their previous journey.

However, the aim was to first reach the northern part of the island. They rested for some time and stocked the canoe. When they reached the shores, they could see some vessels in the distance. Maybe some fishing boats but it was better to be cautious. Then suddenly, they saw a boy in the woods. He too seem surprised and wanted to run away. But the boys motioned for him to stay put and surprisingly the latter did. He seemed to think that the two were from some other settlement in the same island. They spoke and Tibo could understand his tongue, though it had a different accent. The Shompen boy found it difficult since he had not mastered Nicobarese completely.

The boy spoke about his settlement which was not far from the spot. He even wanted to take his new friends there. But the two refrained. They were not sure of the response since some of the tribe elders could be aggressive. They gave the boy some fruits from the canoe. He was happy and started conversing more. The topic was their lifestyle and the boys were surprised that most what he said was also part of the lifestyle of their settlement. Hunting animals like pigs and monkeys with the occasional catch of even crocodiles. Eating of the pandanus fruits and use of its leaves for making homes. etc etc. Not much had changed despite the distance of the islands. When the boy enquired, the two told them about their epic journey and the purpose of it. He looked at them with a wide gap, something akin to seeing celebrities. The boy soon bid them goodbye and agreed not to tell his family about the two. He too was unsure of how the elders would react to the situation. He was witness to some fights between the settlements in the island. He also told the boys to be careful of the outsiders who had taken their forest land. That was a surprising statement from the boy.

After bidding adieu, the boys then got onto their canoe and started their journey to one end of the island. No vessels were visible and they moved along the shores. The waters were a bit choppy but they managed to travel at a good speed. It took some time since the contour of the island was elongated. On the way, they could see some settlements. However, it seemed more to be semi-permanent structures made of brick and mortar. A couple of persons came out of one of these structures but they didn't seem concerned. After all they may have thought that these were indigenous Nicobarese fishing. There were sturdy fishing vessels berthed on the mangroves. These too did not seem to be ones made of natural materials by the indigenous people. They reached the other end and then came ashore at a suitable spot. The canoe had to be hidden in a strategic spot. It was time to stock the canoe with edibles before making the next leg of the journey. While there were small islands on the way, the path to Car Nicobar was very far. It they missed these islands or lost the general direction of the northernmost island of the Nicobar chain, it could take them probably more than a day. They decided to rest for the night and then move at the break of dawn.

It was a clear beautiful morning as the sunrays hits the canoe on which they were soundly sleep. Not even the mosquito bites could break them from the deep slumber. They got up, took some time to admire the lovely day and then rushed to complete their ablutions. Within a quick time, they were ready to leave. A challenging day ahead of them. As they hit the waters, they could see some fishermen venturing out into the sea. Up ahead some distance, were the silhouette of a large ship. The two avoided the fishermen boats and went out into the open sea in the general direction of Car Nicobar. The sky was clear and it was a picture perfect day. It was now that the geography of the islands was important and both of them knew that there were two islands on the way to their destination. And unless they went in the right direction, they would not hit these two. As they moved forward, the waters became a bit choppy but not of much concern. However, the progress was slowed down and they were expending a lot of energy. They could see some fishing vessels in the distance and this brought some relief that they may not be far from land. More importantly, they had not strayed from the landmass they left and the sightings were a sign that they were in the right direction. One of the fishing vessels was curious and came close but then after seeing the boys left. It did not seem to be that of the indigenous people since it was a larger vessel.

No sooner had they made some progress that they sighted land. It was on their left which meant that they had veered towards the right and entering open waters. It was the Sanenya island, whose name the boys were unaware of as it was not mentioned in the map. However, with what was taught in school, they realised that the direction was fine. There was a decision to be taken as to whether they should touch base on the island. After taking into account the situation and their physical condition, they decided otherwise. The plan was to reach another small island before dusk. They had to go around the relatively small island and then move ahead into open waters. It had a lot of vegetation and some beacheads too. However, they kept their distance and circled around it.

The distance to the next island would be much longer and the boys had no time to lose. Once they reached the northern head of the island, they started rowing faster into the open waters. They had to reach their destination in time. They saw more vessels in the distance. Good progress was being made as the canoe went towards its intended destination. Soon, the sun was overhead and beating down. They had to take shelter in some leaves on board. In the forests, they always had adequate shade but here in the open waters, it was a different proposition. They soon took a break for eating something. There was adequate stock on board. They cooled themselves by splashing some water on their bodies. But it was only a temporary relief as the weather elements were harsh. They rested for some time, a sort of a power nap and then began to row. The sea seemed calmer now but the horizon was clear barring a couple of vessels in the distance.

With the renewed energy, they started rowing. They soon left the image of the island they bypassed behind. As the afternoon progressed, the weather elements were kinder and the speed increased. The two boys were eager to sight land before dusk. However, given the distance, it was not going to be easy. And at their speed. It was willy nilly impossible. Dusk soon fell and the boys were scouting the horizon. The Shompen boy saw some light but then they realised that it was that of a vessel. They were disheartened and continued rowing. Soon night fell but the sky was clear. The stars and the moonlight guided their way. The water in the night were calmer but there was an eerie feeling to it. They were feeling a bit drowsy but continued with their efforts. With the passage of time, it became clear to the two that they were still far off from their destination. They had underestimated the distance and were off the mark. So they decided to take on some nutrition at this unearthly hour. It was important to refuel and get their energy flow up.

The rowing resumed with some vigour. With the experience of having done one earlier, the boys were not overawed. Timo was the first one to give way and wanted to rest. His friend then took over the reins to paddle his way forward. They then took turns during the whole night but there was not a speck of light. There were no other vessels too at this time. It was certain that they were all alone. With the passage of time, dawn broke and still no land in sight. The boys realised that they needed to go on. They were however optimistic of finding the island and the vessel trudged ahead. The sunrise was pretty and both of them admired it. It was a break from the monotony of seeing the water. The direction of the sun gave them comfort that they were moving in the right direction. They took another break for refreshments. The boys were feeling a bit groggy with the efforts during the night. They slept off briefly and awoke to the cry of a gull. This was a sign that land was not far off. They rowed in the direction of the bird. It took them another hour before they sighted a small speck of land. There was a tall man made structure which was a lighthouse. As usual, they were not aware of the name but this was Battimalv island. As they moved closer to the island, it seemed small and the structure seemed quite large. There was shrubbery and they could see a canoe parked in the distance. They knew that this was as tiny island and they needed to rest. By the time they hit the shores, it was noon as the sun had climbed overhead. The boys had made an epic journey and had developed confidence to now row in the night. Two such instances were enough for that.

As soon as they hit the island, they just slumped. There was no energy left even to tow the canoe to a safe spot. They assumed the place was uninhabited and just went off to doze on the canoe. When they woke up, it was getting to be dusk. They were hungry and quickly gobbled up the stock in the canoe. They had to now search the place for fresh stock and fresh water. The island was small but the vegetation fairly thick. It was difficult to traverse the woods but with all their experience back home, they soon got the hang of it. The progress was however slow. As soon as it became dark, it was difficult to see around. But they were in luck as they heard the flow of a stream and went in that direction.

The stream was pretty small but there was a flow and it eventually went into a large water body. It didn't seem very clean but the boys just lapped up whatever they could. It was like an oasis in the middle of a desert. They quenched their thirst to heart content. It was time now to look for stocking up. They could see some berries but were not sure if they were edible. Anyhow, they plucked it. Then while retracing, they saw the good old pandunus fruits hanging. With the energy they could muster, they plucked that too. This was good enough for the night and probably their next day journey. They returned to the canoe and decided to hide it in the vegetation.

The effect of the rowing was clearly visible since the hunger persisted. They ate up nearly all the stock they gathered and once again slumped off. Nothing could disturb them as they got up only when the first sunrays hit the canoe. They first noticed a number of ants crawling on the canoe and even their bodies. It seemed that the place was pristine with no sign of human habitation. The boys had to shake off the creepy crawlers before deciding what to do next. It was time for freshening up and then gathering more stock before the long journey ahead. This was going to be the longest part with the big island quite a distance away. The weather was cloudy though the clouds didn't seem to be rainbearing. But somehow the instinct of the Shompen boy, despite staying in the interiors of the island, was to avoid getting into the sea today. Tibo was not convinced and seemed to suggest, "We would never be able to start if we get afraid of the sea. I have gone with the elders even during rough weather and nothing happened." Kayat thought over, "*There are no elders with us and we don't know if this canoe can withstand the rough seas. Let us wait for another day. We also need some rest since the next journey may take us more than a day.*"

The Nicobarese boy was not convinced but then he decided to go along with his friend. Since it was a long journey, he did not want any of them to have any doubts. Moreover, with his medical condition, he was not sure that this should be risked. They had to go as a team. So they decided to stay for another day and take some rest. Somehow the instinct turned out true. The sky suddenly became cloudy and it began to pour. The Nicobarese boy them looked at his friend and said, "*You were right. It was risky going out in this weather. We could have been in trouble.*" They could observe the rough seas and took shelter under some trees. The light had suddenly faded and it seemed that dusk had settled in. It was then that they saw the lights on the structure lit up. It was for the first time that they had seen a lighthouse and were looking at it.

"*Let us see what it is*", said the Nicobarese boy. However Kayat was not sure, "*there may be the outsiders or even some indigenous people. It may not be safe to go*". However, since his friend had agreed with him earlier not to venture into the sea, he saw it as his responsibility to agree to this suggestion. The proposition also seemed less risky since it was unlikely that the people they would not harm the two boys in this island in the middle of nowhere. They waited for the rains to stop. So they slept off again. It seemed that their well oiled biological clock had been shaken up and disrupted. As soon as they woke up, they were confronted by an indigenous man who was staring at them. He had a spear in his hand but did not threaten them. While the danger of the stormy sea had been weathered, this new danger confronted the two.

The man spoke in Nicobarese and Tibo responded. He did not want to hide anything and told them about the plan of the two. He was bemused and could not believe what he was hearing. "*You boys have come all the way from Great Nicobar island. I have only heard of that island and never ever seen it in my life. Are you mad? You could have died in the sea.*" He took them to the lighthouse where they were other members of the settlement. They were all well dressed up unlike the boys. Despite their physical similarities, their lifestyle looked more akin to the foreigners. But it was clear that they were still relatively isolated in the few islands around them and had not ventured outside like some of their kimn. They too could not believe the story of the two boys. One of the elders even told the boys to go back since it was dangerous. However, most were in awe of the two. They cross checked some details of the other nearby islands to make sure that the story was indeed credible.

When asked about the journey, one of the men who had gone to Car Nicobar said that it was a long journey and would take more than a day. However, he said, "*you will find a number of other vessels on the way and in case of any danger, just row towards them and seek help*". This was not too reassuring since in case of any emergency, there would be little time to respond in the high seas. The settlement had some children of their age who were looking at their two peers with amazement. It was almost like a couple of celebrities had visited them. The men showed them the lighthouse which was manned by some of them who were taught by outsiders.

They all had some dinner, the first proper meal for the two after some days of their journey. There were discussions of the culture and way of life of these indigenous people who were also Nicobarese. Being a small island, it was a bit different since the number of animals in the forests were limited. Hence, they relied more on the sea and fish was a stable part of their diet. The settlements were semi-permanent unlike theirs and there was provision of water and electricity. It was just that the tribe still stayed within a forest. Many of the locals also worked in the lighthouse and taken up dressing like the outsiders. They shared some of their stock of food with the boys. The man who had sailed to the Car Nicobar island then came with them to the canoe. He told them about the general direction that they should take the next day early in the morning. The sky was also clearing and the storm had subsided. The boys were all refreshed with the eagerness to undertake the long journey ahead.

They had a good sleep with all the food. Their biological clock was a bit restored as they woke up early in the morning. After freshening themselves, they were surprised to see the elder who had asked the boys to return. He came with some stock off food and wished them well. It seemed that he too was proud of the courage of the boys to undertake this adventure. The boys then put the canoe in water and started off in the direction they were told. It was a perfect day, a far cry from the rainy weather a day back. In the distance, they could see some fishing canoes and some larger vessels. With time, the island behind them disappeared. It was anyhow too small and even the lighthouse was not visible. They rowed with all the energy gathered from the rest undertaken and food had over the previous day. Soon it became warmer with the sun directly overhead. They rested briefly and then began their next phase. There was no time to lose as this was the longest part of the journey. Some vessels were still visible and they assumed that the direction was correct. The weather gods were kind and visibility was also quite significant. However, there was no sight of any land. The progress was relatively much better than their previous high sea journey. All the experience had put them in good stead.

Time passed by and they were oblivious of it. Only when the sun was overhead and was beating down did they realise the passage of time. It was time for a quick break but both of them were not very hungry. The decisions to rest for a day and meet the indigenous people who were supportive and gave them some nourishments were in hindsight the right ones to make. The boys were maturing into adventurists and were actually enjoying it. They saw a vessel in the distance but avoided going too close. Only after a couple of hours when the it was late in the afternoon did they rest and took on some refreshments. The food given by the tribesmen was still tasty after a day and they relished it like home made food. There were some clouds but none too worry. Or so the boys thought.

They began their journey after a well earned rest. But the fatigue of continuous rowing was showing now as they had not taken adequate rest during the day. But they laboured on, slowly and steadily towards their destination. Dusk was slowly setting in but the boys were not worried. The only signs of some concern were the clouds overhead which were getting thicker. Slowly the sun set over the horizon and the boys took a break to admire mother nature. Out in the sea, it was a different feeling altogether. But they could not see the ball of fire go down over the horizon as it was masked by some clouds. Now that was a source of concern for the boys.

No sooner did it become dark that they could see the heavy clouds overhead. It was pitch dark and the two were not used to such conditions in the sea. They were however not fazed and continued to make progress. In such conditions, there was no sign of any light. Then the inevitable happened. It was a downpour. Not so heavy but yet one which could test the strength of their canoe. One of them was busy removing water from the canoe so that it did not destabilise. Slowly as it became a but heavy, both of them were engaged in the same. They covered the boat with some leaves but had to remove the excess water. Fortunately, there were pores from which the water was getting to the sea and the canoe did not overfill. The rains however did not last long. It was however a scary phase to have rains in the middle of the open waters. They were just hoping for it to stop and that it did. As if nature was kind to the two who had embarked on this arduous journey.

But the conditions were difficult as it remained cloudy. There was no light from the moon or stars to guide them. They were just moving ahead in pitch darkness hoping to see some light ahead. There were no vessels in this weather too. The canoe ploughed on, slowly and steadily in the direction which the man had guided them. Therefore, they got some assurance that were moving towards the large island. Sometime later, the two rested and took a small nap. The surrounding lapping of the water prevented them from oversleeping despite the desperation. Maybe back in the land, they would have got up only late in the morning when the sunrays hit down. The two co-ordinated well and managed to stick to their task as the first rays of dawn filtered from over the clouds. There was still no land in sight though the view became clearer with the light. The two did not nurse any fear and there was a palpable feeling that the sea was part of their lives. Their whole existence from birth in the dense woods seemed a thing of the past. The boys were in a way getting acclimatised to the water around them.

As the sun rose over the horizon, the boys saw it on the right side coming from the east. This was a source of comfort for them and they were headed in the right direction. After a good wash with sea water, the two rested to take in some of the food still leftover in the canoe. It was wet from the rains in the evening before but still edible. They ate to their heart full since their destination was still far off. After that, there was the temptation to have a nap but they resisted it since the aim was to cover as much distance as possible when it was daylight. They coaxed each other to continue with the efforts. As they scanned the horizon, there was nothing visible. There seemed to be a large vessel in the distance but the two could not recognise anything as, whatever it was, seemed very far off. The Shompen boy even said that it could be just their hallucination and hope.

Anyhow, after covering some distance, they saw some fishing vessels. It was noon now and the sun was almost overhead.The boys had not taken any rest and did not want to waste time and spend another night in the open waters. They were lucky that the downpour last night was not torrential. These vessels were a sign that the people on board were from the large island. So they decided to go near one of the vessels. The people on board saw the approaching canoe and looked in that direction. When they reached at a reasonable distance, they could make out that these were indigenous people fishing in the morning hours. They had made a good catch. On inquiry, the boys said that they were coming from the small island and were looking for Car Nicobar. The three men on board were in a literal shock to see the two boys having come such a long distance. One of them had made the distance to that island but it had taken him and his companions around two days to do it. Moreover, the weather had been inclemental with the rains but yet they had reached the destination. These boys had just spent one night and here they were not far away from the large island. Both the boys understood what the men said as they directed them to go in a particular direction to reach the island. However, they warned them of being cautious. The continued with the fishing after giving the directions to the boys.

The two then went along at a good speed. Meeting the fishermen had infused some confidence in them that they would reach land. However, now the boys did not have that same yearning for land as was when they set out. They were comfortable in the watery surroundings. But they had to reach their destination. Soon, they sighted land but were more reserved in their celebrations. It was time for pragmatism. One of the most difficult part of their journey lay ahead of them. It was crossing a wide channel to get to the Little Andamans. Virtually impossible in this canoe. The landscape was picturesque as the treeline came into full view. This was definitely a large island as they neared it. It was not time to look for a good spot to berth. There were many fishing vessels, beaches and rocky outcrops on the island. They were looking for an isolated place so as not to attract attention. They started circling around the island. It took them some time to find a place meeting the isolation parameter. There were many fishing vessels on the way and some of them were curious seeing the two boys.

They had finally reached the last of the Nicobarese islands. From here the more difficult part of their journey would begin. And more importantly ridden two rough weather conditions in the sea and come out unscathed. "*Fortune favours the brave*" was the right adage for the journey of the two boys.

****

CHAPTER XI

Welcome to the Islands

After berthing their vessel, it was time to hide it in the woods. They probably would not use it for their further journey but needed it on the way back. But only if they came out of all this unscathed. It had been a long journey and the two were tired. They rested and dozed off. By the time they got up, it was dusk. It wasn't the appropriate time to go into the woods but they needed to drink some water. So they trudged into the thick undergrowth, picked up some berries on the way and found a stream. All with the help of sounds as the forest was dark. After quenching their thirst and washing themselves, it was time to return. They had a hearty meal with whatever was left on the canoe. Food from the last two days but they found it very palatable given that they were famished from the arduous journey. Finally, it was time to sleep again. The exertion made them doze off and they woke up early next day. The skies were clear but there was a lot of activity in the sea. A number of fishing vessels were in the sea. There was a large vessel carrying people and it gave a hoot. Tibo had seen such vessels from his settlement and knew that these were passenger ferries. The Shompen boy had not seen one at this distance since they had avoided going close to vessels during the time spent in the deep waters. It moved fairly fast compared to their canoe. He was staring at in amazement. Some of the people on board noticed them too. They waved at the boys.

The first piece of the puzzle was to find help on the next leg of the journey. It was not going to be easy since they probably needed to board one of those ferries to reach the Andamans. How would they manage that with nothing in hand. Probably, they needed the help of some indigenous people. But there was no guarantee that they would get the support. Anyhow, they went into the woods to find the stream. The forests were not as dense and hence they found it easier to traverse. The water source was found and they washed themselves and ate some berries on the trees. Slowly they were ready to move. It was decided that they would try to establish contact with some indigenous people. Tibo was of the view that the people may be closer to the sea as they would be dependent on fish. But soon they found a settlement.

One of the men guarding it came with an aggressive intent with a spear. "*Stop, we are friends*", was the instinctive response of the Shompen boy. The man was surprised at the features of the boy since he had not seen a Shompen. Tibo jumped in and said "*We are were just boys who have come from far and want to talk to the elders.*" The man was initially hesitant but relented when he saw that they were not a threat. He took them to the elder of the settlement. The conversation was on how the boys got here and what was their plan. There was nothing to hide. First the elder was suspicious about the story but when they told about their sea journey, he was surprised at their bravado in undertaking such a risky journey. His first response was "*Why didn't you tell your families about it.*" The boys did not respond directly. The Shompen boy then said "*We want to travel and see our islands. Our parents would not have allowed us if we had told them.*"

The elder was surprised but also took note of the candour of the boy. He was still stunned by the tale of crossing so many islands which were all fraught with danger. No one among the indigenous people had ever the audacity to undertake it. But here were two youngsters, all willing to take these risks for crossing the islands and finding about the other indigenous people. He quickly made up his decision without consulting anyone. He came to the point and said, "*The distance from this island to the Little Andamans, the next stop is very far. Even our big canoe's haven't crossed it. You would have to take one of the large passenger vessels for that. We can give you money for the two tickets on the vessel and something to eat. After that you two are on your own.*"

The boys were overjoyed. They could now hit the Andaman's, probably the toughest part of their journey. But the question that came to the elders mind was, "*How will we get two tickets for them? They did not have any identification*". With the sensitivity of the islands, the authorities were generally strict and it would be difficult to get someone on board without proper identification. Tibo could still pass off as one of them but the Shompen boy with his distinctive features would stand out. So it was decided that they would take a local vessel of one of the Nicobarese and cross over to the Little Andaman's. It would take more time but was safer since the owners were known to them. The vessel was to sail only the day after. So the elder invited the two to stay in his settlement.

The boys could see that the tribesmen looked more integrated into mainstream society. They wore modern clothes and even had permanent structures. In the discussions, they came to know that some of them had left the settlement for small towns. Some had taken up jobs there and were reluctant. A few of them had built permanent structures for their families. Even most of the food was being got from outside and the people rarely went for hunting. Fishing and collecting of fruits were still important and this was a daily ritual. They discussed the customs and practises. Many of these were the same as that of Tibo's settlement but there were some differences accentuated by the migration and travel of many of them to the urban and semi-urban centres in the island. Things like the belief in ghosts and spirits seemed to have mitigated. Families were also smaller since the youngsters were slowly moving out.

The boys decided to help the community in food gathering and fishing. They went with a group of men to collect fruits. The forests were not as dense and there was a pathway too. They came across some pandanus fruits and just plucked them. The size was slightly smaller than the one back home. They reached a road and there were some vehicles on it. They gave some of the fruits to some people, who seemed to outsiders in the passing vehicles. Some money was exchanged for this. Kayat were surprised to see the level of interaction of the Nicobarese with the locals. Back home they were relatively isolated from the others and had their own lives in the deep forests.

Back from the forests, the homes where they ate and slept were also very different. There was electricity and taps with the structure being more permanent made of bricks and mortar. It seemed a different world for him. For Tibo, the exposure to the outside world was more significant and he felt less surprised. He had visited some of his relatives who lived with all such amenities. The food was more elaborate and well cooked with rice, lentils, vegetables. It was all served in metallic vessels. The two were just admiring the menu in front of them and ate to their heart content. The elder was looking at them with amusement, "*Looks like you haven't eaten anything in days. Missing your home food*", he laughed. The boys did not listen as they were busy filling their stomachs.

They had a deep sound sleep. The journey had been exhausting. They woke up early morning all freshened up. There was another day at rest before they boarded the vessel for the Andamans. So it was decided that they would go on one of the fishing expeditions. They climbed onto a canoe and went into the sea. The direction was towards the Andamans and the men were planning to go into the deep sea. They had harpoons to spear the fish and were planning to get a big catch. They used bamboo sticks with the iron spear at one end. The canoe was sturdier than the one they traversed the open waters. The pace was also much faster and they soon entered the deep sea. "This is the direction of the Little Andamans and it would take us a whole day to reach there", said the skipper of the vessel. The boys could see that the fishermen were always keeping a lookout for the clouds in the sky. When he saw the boys were curious, one of them remarked, "*In the open sea, one never knows how the weather may change. Any sign of rains, the sea will be stormy and it is better to turn back.*"

When the boys told about their rendezvous with the rains, the skipper remarked, "*It is foolish to be in the deep sea at that time. You never know when a wave can topple your canoe. It is then difficult to correct the vessel when the waves are so high. Only luck can then save you.*" The boys imbibed those words of wisdom. They knew that they had made some bad decisions. But then this was new to them and no one had ever taught them the rules when sailing into the sea. One of the men pointed to a speck of cloud in the horizon. The skipper just remarked, "*Both of you boys keep a lookout for that cloud. If it nears this place or turns heavy, tell us.*" The boys were disappointed. They had come here to help out the men with their fishing and here they were being told to watch out for the clouds. The skipper could sense their disappointment. He remarked. "*We work here as a team. Each of us has a specific task. Your task is equally important as that of the actual fishing. If you don't forewarn us in time, we all might be doomed.*"

The cloud did not threaten to be of any concern. It remained far away and did not form into that dreaded rain bearing one. The boys could then see how the men were sharpening the ends of their harpoon. The men pointed to some fish skimming the surface of the water. The boys had never noticed that when they were out on the sea. It required some discerning eyes for that. While one of them kept a watch on the clouds, the other looked at the water surface. The men were now ready with their harpoons. They neared the canoe to a large shoal and then one of them stood up at the front and swung the spear into the water while holding one end tight. With the skill garnered over the years, it hit its mark and pierced through. The man skilfully pulled out the harpoon and along it came a large catch. The boys recognised it as a tuna, fairly significant in size. Even Tibo had not seen his tribesmen make such a high sea catch. They caught fish in relatively shallower waters. The other men then subdued the oversized fish on the vessel as it splayed its body around. When the movements became less, the man pulled out the spear. Meanwhile, one of the other men had also harpooned another fish, this time a barracuda.

The boys were surprised to see the large shoals moving beneath the boat. The men were also baiting them with some powder. This was a concoction made back home by grinding some fruits and nuts. Slowly, they started spearing more fish and the catch was impressive. Both of them wanted to join in and the men allowed them. They were able to catch a fish each and were thrilled. It was a new experience for them in the open waters. It would be helpful in their journey ahead. Finally, after a couple of hours in the sea, the men rested for some refreshments. It was a social gathering and the men told about the tales. There were instances of people falling overboard and rescued, some shark attacks, encounters with poisonous sea snakes, being caught in a light storm and encounters with large shipping and passenger vessels that came too close for comfort. The men were however more keen on the adventures of the boys. They were surprised that the two had made this perilous journey from the comforts of their home, all with the purpose of meeting the indigenous people of the islands. Time passed so fast and they decided to resume their fishing. This time they were not so successful probably because the fish shoals were no longer trailing their vessel. The baits also did not seem to work. Maybe it was warmer and this kept the marine creatures away. With the little success, the men allowed the boys to do the fishing. Both of them did it with enthusiasm and managed to catch some. The men appreciated it and then decided to call it a day. It was late afternoon and they needed to reach the shores before dusk. They rowed their way back, albeit at a slower pace due to the strain put in during the day. It took some time before they sighted land again. Then they moved ahead and berthed at the right spot. There were some vessels in the background and some men on the shores. All of them were from the settlement and were waiting for the vessel. They were shocked at the catch. It seemed as if this was one of the better days despite the lull after the break. Ine of them said, "*Looks like the boys brought you some luck.*". One of the fishermen responded, "*Yes and they helped us too. They are good at this work despite not having much experience*". The boys were overjoyed at this compliment.

After they reached back to the shore, they went to the settlement. The elders had prepared a celebration for the boys. They were overcome with tears of joy as the entire settlement had gathered for a feast. There was an elaborate array of dishes including their favourite pork. This overwhelmed them more since it seemed like the last such feast was ages ago. The journey had made them forget time. But first there was the traditional Nicobarese dance. Young men and women dressed in their traditional attire took centrestage. For Tibo, this was a recollection of the dance back home in his settlement. However, it was less elaborate and colourful than this one. He found the Car Nicobar culture a bit different from the one on this island. It may have got to do with the increased level of interaction with the outsiders and the proximity to the Andamans. In his settlement, the colours were less prominent and costumes were less elaborate. But one could not rule out the occasion too as the boys never expected such a welcome.

Finally, they coaxed the boys to join in the dance. They were given the same set of costumes too. Tibo was well versed with the steps and managed to gel in. Kayat fell a bit uneasy as he had not participated in such a large dance troupe. He slowly studied it and then joined in. The other dancers focussed more him given his different features. There was a time when he was surrounded by the girl dancers and he felt a bit shy and overwhelmed. It was all in good spirit and some elders also joined in. As the beats grew louder the speed of the movements also enhanced and the dancers also went into a frenzy. The boys slowly synchronised with the dancers and matched with the beats. There were a number of songs played and both of them had a great time. They were asked to take a break but there were in a way sucked into the beats and did not relent. It was humid and sweat started to pour but this did not wane the enthusiasm. They did not have this type of a vigourous exercise for quite some time and this was an opportunity. There was a lot of clapping and shouting by the dancers and this egged them on. The settlement folks were happy to see the boys so enthusiastic. There was a bonding and the two were seen as heroes trying to understand the culture of their land.

Then it was time for the feast. All of them sat on the ground and food was served. The boys were literally gobbling it up and the elders looked at in amusement. It was a sign that they had indeed made a long perilous journey from their settlement. They ate to their hearts full. Probably like the last supper before their embarked on the difficult part of their journey. The elders came over and first told all those who came about the adventure of the boys. They goaded their youngsters also to be brave like them. The Shompen boy was surprised. His community would have been aghast seeing two boys leaving their settlement and travelling together. For Tibo, probably his parents and elders may have shown less aversion since their level of integration with mainstream society was deeper. Yet his community back home was relatively more isolated than this one. But for the features, the other aspects of their lives were very different and probably the proximity to the Andamans had led to this transformation. However, both were grateful to the community which welcomed them with open arms and gave them the nourishment and encouragement. It also set aside all doubts and apprehensions the two may have nurtured before they set out on this learning adventure.

One of the elders then took the boys to one side. "I need to tell to you something". The facial features of the boys suddenly became a bit grim after all the merriment. "*The tribes in the Andamans are a bit more aggressive than ours. They have lived with and interacted with outsiders and hence there have been conflicts. The Jarawas have known to come into conflict with other people and resisted coming closer. You must already have heard of the North Sentinelese. They are known to be cannibalistic in nature and would not spare you. So I would advise you to be cautious. Do not go to the North Sentinels since it is a matter of life and death there.*" The boys had heard something about all this from their settlements and even in school. They knew the perilious nature of their journey but did not press further. But they were surprised that this man knew so much about the other tribes.

****

CHAPTER XII

The Channel Journey

The next day had clear sunny skies. Ideal for them to embark on their journey across the Ten Degrees Channel into the Andamans. The boatmen were preparing their vessel and packing it with stuff like pandanus, coconuts, bananas. All to sell in the Little Andamans where it fetched a better price. The boys washed themselves and stocked themselves with provisions. The vessel ride was the easier part. It was the navigation after that which would test their mettle. The vessel then moved out from the waters of the Car Nicobar. There was a wide expanse of sea in front of them. The vessel was much faster than their canoe and there were more men on board to lend a helping hand. Even the boys joined as it cut its way through the waters. The experience was exhilarating as the boys had not witnessed such speed. Along the way, the weather was good with clear skies and the conditions were not windy. All this helped in the navigation. There were other vessels also plying ranging from small canoes for who were fishing to passenger vessels. The crew also saw a large container ship passing. This was something that none of the boys and even the men on board had not seen. They were looking at the containers loaded on the large vessel. It took them around a good ten hours to sight the Andamans. There were a lot of vessels in the proximity including the fast passenger vessels. If they had sailed alone, it may have taken them a good two days and nights.

The landing was on a chosen berth and the men quickly unloaded their stuff. They planned to go to a market to sell their produce the next day. They would use the vessel as the place for them to sleep in the night and then leave the day after that. This was a routine for them. The boys volunteered to help and the men were happy. Any extra hand was an asset to them since there was a lot of work like loading, unloading, setting up shop. The night went off peacefully on the boat and they all went into a deep sleep. As dawn hit, they all got up and went into their routine. They then gathered for taking their produce to the nearby market. The market was fairly crowded and there was a beehive of humanity. They put all their wares onto a cloth and were preparing for customers. They were in luck as people flocked to their place. Kayat saw how money was being exchanged for the produce. He had some basic knowledge of counting since people in the settlement relied upon him. He used it to good effect and was quickly looking after the monetary transactions. There were phases when the prices were raised given the demand. The market place economy was in full swing and the boys got a first hand experience of mercantilism. Finally, the goods were sold in a jiffy and the men were also surprised at their luck. There were days when they had to go back with unsold goods at the end of the day. It seemed that there was an upcoming festival and the demand was high. They also had the perception that the boys had got them good luck. They rewarded them with some money and food. However, they were unaware of the more difficult part of their journey, finding out the indigenous people on the island, chiefly the Onges.

So they bid farewell. It was an emotional one since the boys had established a bond with them in the limited period of stay. It however seemed a long period and they now considered them as part of their kin. Even the differently featured Shompen boy. There was sense of apprehension since they knew that life would not be easy for the boys amidst the language barrier and the aggressive nature of some of the indigenous tribes. They could only wish that the boys returned safely after accomplishing their mission. Finally, the boys were on their own. It was important for them to take stock and decide on the way forward.

****

CHAPTER XIII

Meeting the Onges

The first thought was the modus operandi to find the Onges. For this they knew that some help was required. One of the ideas that came was to find some Nicobarese, some of those who had stayed back in the island. However, this could also run them into trouble given the difference in physical features of the two tribes. However, they were taught that the tribe was slowing interacting with outsiders and were getting integrated. However, the level of interaction was not as much as the Nicobarese.

This was the first time that the boys would interact with the tribes from the Negrito family. The boys had landed in the South bay, the southern most part of the island and knew that the tribes were in the forests of this region. Whatever it was they were getting into unchartered territory with no certainty of the reception they would get. But as they say "*fortune favours the brave*". So they rested that night on the sea shore. There was no canoe so it has to be on some logs of wood covered with leaves. More importantly, it had to be away from the water. The high tide was a factor that they had to take into account.

When they woke up in the morning, the sky was clear and the water exuded various shades of blue and green. The sandy shores were clean. They quickly washed themselves in the sea water and decided to make for the woods. No sooner had they done this, they spotted a boy around their age coming from the undergrowth towards the sea. All three of them were startled. The boy was short and dark with features very similar to what they had heard about the Onges. It was a eureka moment for the boys as it was an encounter of serendipity. The boy initially decided to rush back but the two addressed them first in Nicobarese. He did not understand the words but could gauge that the two did not seem like the outsiders. He did not run and stood his ground. The boy came close and queried, "*Where are you from? Can you take us to your settlement?*". The boy did not seem to understand them but replied in broken Hindi, "*I am from this place. Who are you?*". The boys were conversant with the language and told him about themselves. They expressed their desire to reach the settlement and said that they came from the Nicobar islands. The boy was surprised. He had not met someone with their complexion and one who had travelled so far. Initially he was hesitant. With some coaxing and seeing that they were boys of his age, he asked them to follow him.

They went through some dense woods. It was very much like back home and the two were comfortable navigating the terrain. After a good walk, they reached an open area in which there were some huts. The boy called out and some people came out of the settlement. There were all short with dark features. They saw the two boys and called out others too. They all came out and surrounded the boys. The boy seemed to say something to them and this calmed them down. It was obvious from the features that these were Onges. One of them came forward and asked the boys the same question, "*Who are you and where have you come from?*" Nothing was hidden in the response provided. The men were in shock. They had never met someone who travelled so far. The boys were also observing the features of the tribe, specifically their short height and dark features. Some of them had a white colour painted on their faces. It was scary in the first instance for anyone. The men were also curious about the complexion of the boys. One of them went close and touched one of the boys. It was a comical examination of the features as they had not seen each other. They laughed in amusement at all this.

Then they examined some of the houses. These were on stilts with some distance from the ground. It was made of bamboo and there was a ladder to climb up to the floor of the house. Some dogs suddenly came from under the floor and started barking at the boys. These were the guardians of the settlement and the boys had to be wary. The Shompen boy was more confident and had a way with animals back home. He just kept his nerves and stared at the couple of dogs. The animals got the message and then came close to him. They smelt him and Tibo who was of course a bit shaken up and not sure of the response to these animals. One of them asked, "*Why did you leave your families? It is a dangerous to go out in the open seas. And not all tribes are friendly like ours. They may even kill you.*"

The boys had heard this advise before. They were not fazed. Kayat responded, "*We want to understand the different cultures of our land. The open seas do not scare us and we are confident of going further up the Andamans. We would like to meet all the indigenous people to give us a better perspective of the customs and traditions of the islands.*" The man was impressed and he translated it to his fellowmen. One elder then got up and examined the boys. He put his hand on both of them as if blessing them. Then tears came in his eyes as he told the other men, "*I have never seen such brave boys. Willing to risk their lives in the open sea to learn more about people like us. They are our guests and we must honour them.*" So the welcome in this settlement was also unexpected for the boys. They were lulled into a comfort zone in their first encounter with a tribe in the Andamans.

Everyone in the settlement was curiously examining the boys. Some of them even touched them while others looked on in amusement as if they were examining a species from a museum. Communication was a problem since very few spoke Hindi. So it was all in sign language. But it was a moment of bonding for the community. The boys decided to talk about the other tribes in the region and explain to the people in the settlement about the unique cultural ethos of the island. This was necessary to provide a broader perspective of the islands that they inhabited.

There was a language barrier. However, Kayat was smart and picked up some words of Onge. So he mixed up words so as to make himself more receptive to the audience. It was a bit comical and generated some laughter. But the elders were happy that the boy was making an effort to strike a chord with them. The children of their age were quite participative and even managed to ask some questions. After all they connected being in the peer group. Some of the adventurous ones were curious about the journey. They also asked about the school and what was taught there.

Finally, it came down to brass-tacks. How would they cross into the main islands of the Andamans? The elders were awed at the confidence level of the boys. They could not fathom how two youngsters could be so dare devilish in their approach without caring for all the troubles that might come in their path. One of them asked, "*what is the food that you eat back home to be so brave?*" The others laughed. But no one had any idea at that moment on how the boys could be helped to achieve their goal. Anyhow, it was time for the tribesmen to explain some things about the Onges and their way of life. The first thing that came up was the colour of their skin. Being dark complexioned, it was obvious that they came from a different place compared to the Nicobarese and the Shompens. Then one of the old men warned the boys about the diseases that the outsiders had brought with them. "*You must be careful. Many of our forefathers died due to this. We are dwellers of the forests and seas*". They talked about their hunting and fishing skills including the ability to go out in the open seas. "*The sea may be dangerous but there are always clues about the weather and you need to respect it. Even on a sunny day, if you see some clouds on the horizon, don't venture out. The sea can be very unforgiving on those who test it. We have lost so many of our fishermen to the waters. It is the spirits that protect us and we need to pray to them.*" The boys understood that spirits seemed to be an important part of their lives.

Finally, it was time for some meals. The settlement brought in some dishes for all to share. The boys were asked to join in. They were initially hesitant but joined in. It was elaborate with pork, sweet potato, honey and even rice. The boys were hungry and ate to their hearts full. It was like a big family as the men, women and children all joined in. No rocket science as to who were at the centre of attraction. Many from the tribe hadn't seen indigenous people of Mongoloid origin. Even the boys were surprised at the colourful attires and paints on the faces of the tribes. Communication remained an issue but the translator in the group helped out the boys. Some of the teens in the group were eyeing the dress of Tibo. Kayat tried to use some words that he had learnt. It was about a teen talk about life in general. The boys and girls were surprised at the adventure spirit of the two. One of them even asked if he could join them. The elders gave a stern look.

After the meal, everyone washed themselves with some water caught in a vessel. Then they sat down near one of the huts and continued the discussion. One of the elder suddenly said, "*We have fishermen who will go out into the deep sea and to the next island. You can be dropped off there. From there, you would need to look at other vessels to take you further.*" Someone then said, "*if they can wait for another two days, we are going fishing to Rutland island which is close to the main Andamans. It would easier for them to reach the mainland then. We also have our brethren there who can help the boys*" The boys decided to wait out the longer period since that would given them some time to explore this island while taking them closer to their intended destination. There were many small islands on the way but most of these were uninhabited and it would be difficult to get a vessel to move further. The probability of getting one on Rutland island was more.

So the boys decided to explore the Little Andaman's first. There was a hunting expedition going to the forests and the boys joined in. The aim was to first get some honey. It was a long trek through the dense woods. There were a couple of teenagers too, all being roped in to understand the art of collecting the produce. They reached an opening where there were some hives up on the trees. The men covered themselves with some cloth to escape the sting of the bees. They lit a fire and one of them climbed up the tree to the hive and spread the smoke around it. The bees were perturbed by the smoke and quickly scattered in fear. No sooner than the hive seemed empty than one of the men then got a grip on it and squeezed it. Another had a vessel in which he collected it. Some of the bees still left attempted to sting the men but the cloth provided good protection. However, one of the boys on the ground got stung by one of the bees that had dispersed. He let out a yell and one of the men came to check it out. It didn't seem serious and the focus was again on the two men. When one of the men came down, it was a bountiful of the sweet liquid. The men had not disturbed the hive and managed to get what they wanted.

Another set of men then climbed another tree which had another hive. This was larger and the smoke was not enough to disperse the creatures. They decided to squeeze the hive anyhow. It was dangerous with little protection but one of them was experienced. He managed to take out liquid without overtly disturbing the inhabitants of the hive. He was however stung by a few bees in the process but did not flinch. The boys could understand that it was a dangerous proposition. They had helped out back home too but the people in the settlement did not take the type of risk this Onges community was taking. Probably, back home, honey was not as much sought after as here. It was clear that the men were hell bent on taking out whatever honey was available in the hives above. They met with a lot of success but it was a package with stings in good measure. The men however, did not care much for the pain and were willing to take calculated risks. Both Tibo and Kayat helped out in the process with the Shompen boy even climbing one of the trees to hold out the vessel for taking in the nectar. He didn't seem scared of the swarms around him. The men appreciated his bravado. The produce was beyond expectations and it seemed that group had managed to squeeze out all the hives that they could sight. They were in good luck in having spotted so many too. Looked like the bees had laid out a present for them. It was a moment of celebration and the boys joined in. A dance in circles with the pots of honey placed in the centre. The bonding had increased and the boys felt as part of the tribe.

After they returned, the celebrations continued in the settlement. It was more elaborate with the other men, women and children joining in. Many looked at the boys as an elder announced that they had brought them good luck. He touched their forehead as if blessing them. The boys were overwhelmed. They had not done the real physical work of the other men who had to climb and be stung by the bees. Looked like their efforts were being over recognised. But then after all they were outsiders and were happy to have contributed to the effort.

Some fishermen then took the cue and requested the elders to allow the boys to join them in the evening fishing expedition. In the flow of emotion, the elders agreed and the boys were to go. The morning fishing outing had not been a good one and hence the men were forced to go to the sea again. One of the men signalled that the boys would be tired. But the Shompen boy who understood some words was quick to rebut. He said that both of them would go. Tibo lost out on the communication but when it was translated to him, he too agreed. After all where would the boys get all the opportunity to do all this. It would also help them in the adventures that lay ahead.

The men headed out into the open waters. Unlike the boys, they seemed to have thrown caution to the winds. They did not even check out the cloud cover. As they rowed further, one of them pointed at a distance. The boys could make out a silhouette of a land. "*We will get fish closer to that island. It is on the way to Rutland. Let us land there first and pick up some fruits.*" The vessel soon reached the island and they touched shore. The island seemed very small but there was dense forest cover. The man guided others into the undergrowth. It was as if he knew the place at the back of his hand. They reached a stream and all of them cleaned themselves. Then they went further in and they found a group of trees with some berries. The man motioned and others plucked the fruit and tasted it. It was sweet and unlike what the boys had eaten before. They gathered some of it and each of the men took it back to The boat. They loaded all the berries and were now ready to go back to the deep sea for fishing. The boys admired the beauty of the island with its pristine white sand beaches.

The sea was calmer than when they ventured into it. After picking a spot, the men looked down on the fishes. There were some shoals and the boys spotted it. They had both spears as well as bow and arrows. The boys were successful with their aim with the spear and managed to catch some large fish. It was not an easy task in having to spot the shoals below, balance and then throw the weapon with pinpoint accuracy. There was no room for any error. The ones who used bow and arrows were not as successful. It was a decent catch but still below expectations. Fishing was about a lot of luck since once is not sure about the presence of shoals. Nevertheless, the boat was loaded with both fish and the berries. The settlement would be relatively happy with the overall catch if one accounts for the gold pot of honey.

Despite the limited fish catch, there was a generally positivity in the community. The women began preparations for a feast and some of the men joined in. The children were helping out the household in the chores. The two boys also understood their role and they helped in setting the house of the elder in order. They also cleaned up the place where the feast was to be made. Time just passed in all the errands. There was a buzz in the community as everyone was busy with their tasks. There was no need for giving any directions since everyone was clear about their work. It was one community task and they were ready as soon as the sun had set on the horizon.

Finally, it was time for another round of celebrations. What better way than a dance. There was a group that had prepared for this and came out with colourful costumes. The paint on the faces was even more prominent that the normal one. There wore headgear made out of bamboo. The dresses were also adorned with a lot a colour. The women had their own set of costumes which effused vibrancy in all its hues. The dance itself was to the sound of drumbeats. A very lively and rhythmic music with beats that were more vigourous than the one back in their island. Probably the difference in the genesis of the tribes in the Andamans and the Nicobar island chains may have led to this. The dancing went on for some time and the boys had difficult keeping pace with the steps. The Onges seemed to have boundless store of energy bundles and apart from the elders showed little sign of fatigue. It looked like they didn't want it to stop and only when someone called for the feast did not some of the youngsters reluctantly stop their steps.

The spread was sumptuous. The community had taken a lot of efforts in preparing it. There was pork, fish and turtle meat on the menu. On the vegetarian side, there was rice, a vegetable preparation, tubers and some honey. Tea was also served in pots. But due to the vigour of the dance, many were less hungry than thirsty. So it was not like a rush to the food table. More like people gathering their breathe and deciding what to eat. The elders who had rested well were the first to be served. They all ate to heart full. The women and youngsters then had their turn. The boys joined in and tried turtle meat, something they hadn't tasted back home. Even tea was a new drink for them back home though they had seen it in school. With all the fatigue, the appetite was still not there.

It was clear that the community was close knit. The social interaction through such events was a means of increasing that bonding. The boys who were reluctant in the beginning and felt that the tribes were so different from theirs now began nursing thoughts that this was their family. They joined in the festivities with full enthusiasm and vigour. The community too took them as an their own. The colour of the skin and the complexion seemed to a factor of no concern for the Onges community. It was as if they bonding with people who had seamlessly blended into mother nature and were living a sustainable lifestyle. They were not considered outsiders.

The next day, the boys got up early. They refreshed themselves and were ready to help out the community. This time, it was a visit to a tea plantation to pluck leaves. This was an entirely new concept for them and they saw the shrubs growing in an undulating landscape. There were other boys and girls who accompanied them. Not much of a conversation since only the Shompen boy knew some words he had picked up. It was mostly sign language but some of them spoke to the boy. He could understand most of what was told but then had to reply either in this language or use some signs. Tibo was looking at this conversation with a lot of interest and amusement. He too began picking up some words of Onge but didn't have the confidence to use them in conversation.

After reaching the plantations, the boys first observed the others. They then plucked out the leaves which were ripe. It was a difficult task as it was both about observation of the ripe leaves and a long trudge to select the shrubs. They had bamboo baskets on their shoulder. These were all handmade back in the community. Mostly done by women who were expert basket weavers. Akin to what is done in the modern plantations around the country. Finally, they had gathered enough leaves to fill their baskets. They rested for some refreshments of fruits and what else but tea in a pot. Then they made their way back. The boys got to know that the leaves would be cleaned and then put in boiling water to extract the essence. Of course, there was no machinery involved and everything was what was passed down ages. After returning from the collection of leaves, they saw the entire process which was rudimentary. But after all, this was for consumption within the community. Sometimes, they bartered this produce for other essentials from the outsiders.

After returning to the community, it was time to refresh. The Onges then sat down for a communal lunch. It was not as elaborate as the night before. Bare essentials like rice, vegetables and some pork. Some of it was that leftover and it was heated by the women. They talked about the tea plantations. The boys with the little communication talked about the experience of going to the plantations and collecting leaves. It was something new to them and the community gauged the excitement. After the food and the conversation, it was time for a nap. They slept well after the exertion. Once they got up, it was time to go on a hunting expedition. This was to catch some boars. A group of men were readying the bows and arrows as well as spears. Not very different from what was done at home. The men went into a huddle and discussed the strategy. The boys looked at all this from outside. Such discussions were not uncommon in their community too. When this was over, one of the men told the boys that the decision was to go to a particular part of the forests which they had not gone before. Some children had sighted a boar family there while playing. They would split up into four groups and approach from different directions. Going by the location of the family, they would then encircle the place and move inwards towards the target. However, since these animals roamed large tracts of the forest, it was not necessary that they would be there. Some would also try to escape from the trap set through patches in between the groups. But this was a better strategy since otherwise the animal can easily outrun them. The Shompen boy remembered using this strategy once in his island but with little success. It was difficult to predict where the animals would be in the forest.

There were three to four men in each of the groups. All of them were armed with bows, arrows or spears. The boys were also split up into different groups. It was a competitive environment and whoever speared or shot the boar would be felicitated in the community. The groups were thus motivated to be the ones killing the animals. There was a sub strategy being worked out within each of the groups. Kayat's group decided to place two of their strongest men at the front with the boy at the end. On the other hand, the four people in Tibo's group had not such formation. They all went it stealthily into the forest. The animals would be scared away with any sound. All the groups went towards their task. Then suddenly, both the boys heard a shout from one of the groups. It was clear that they had spotted the animal and were chasing it. The peace of the forests was disturbed and so was the strategy. The initial plan was to reach a particular place and then hopefully encircle the boar family. Then they would converge and hone in. However, with this initial shout, all the plans went for a toss. All the groups ran in the direction of the noise in the hope of finding to the animal first. The Shompen boy did mention that the group should approach with caution but in the adrenaline rush, no one was listening. They all ran as if it was a race to catch the animal. Then out of nowhere one of the animals which was nearby charged on Kayat's group. Two of the front men went literally tossed like toys. They gave out a scream that rang through the dense forests. The power of these wild animals was for all to see. They then charged away into the undergrowth. The Shompen boy was however alert and gave chase. From the corner of his eye, he sent one of the arrows in the direction of the animals and there was a loud scream. A bloodcurling scream that signalled the extinguishing of life. He had hit his mark. It may have looked brutal but that was it. The two men were literally dazed and had not time to react. Still recovering from the bruises.

The third man of the group was in a state of shock, not sure whether the admire the feat of the Shompen boy or nurse the wounds of his comrades. He had not seen someone keep his cool, amidst the charge of the boars, and then hit the mark with precision, despite being unsighted. He quickly accompanied Kayat and the subdued the helpless animal with his spear. A cruel end but it was a matter of existence for these indigenous people.

The other group hearing the screams, both human and that of the animal came running in the direction. They rushed to see who managed to kill the animal. They first met the two men who were flung by the charging boars. Sturdy men, albeit unable to withstand the power of this wild animal. The men had still not quite recovered from the shock. It was as if a large creature had smacked them. It was probably their first experience too and were literally shaken up. Normally the animals have a keen sense of hearing. But it was the strategy of encirclement that confused them and forced them to try to bulldoze their way out. Bulldoze they did, with two unlucky Onges in the way.

Then came the bigger surprise. The third man pointed to Kayat and he blurted out, "*He is the one who got the animal*". At first, the others thought it was a joke. How could a boy who did not live in this part of the world, atleast this island, be such a good hunter? And to top it, the situation was so precarious that the two experienced men were flung by the animal. Surely, anyone would have been shocked in such a situation. And to gather one's wits was remarkable. They all looked at the boy with awe and admiration. The boy however, suddenly felt awkward at all this. He had never experienced such a situation in his life. In his island, he was considered a good hunting help. His father used to say, "*this boy has such a keen sense and a calm demeanour*". The elders of his community did praise him on and off but he had not done something like this back home.

Anyhow, he wanted the focus to be off him. So he quickly went to check out on the men for their injuries. Surprisingly, the two were just dazed. There were some bruises but nothing of significance for the type of encounter they had. Probably, life in the wild had taught them about the art of saving themselves from serious injuries. The others then covered the animal with leaves and attached it to bamboo sticks. Four of them carried the animal. They asked the boy to lead them in the long walk back to the village. It was a victory march of sorts but the boy took it as a matter of fact. With his sense of direction, he was soon able to reach the community. As soon as the elder men in the community saw the animal being carried, they let out a shout. They were shocked to see the Shompen boy at the front of the group. It was a place of honour given to the hunter.

Then it was all chaos. Everyone came and hugged the boy. It was as if he had brought them good luck. The hunts over the last week were not so successful and this boy seemed to have changed all that. Tibo was also not left out since both had come together. Both were a bit overawed at the situation. They had merely gone out to help in the hunt with the little experience they had back home. But they were not expecting that one of them would be the one to finally kill the animal. They had never done this back home. Probably never given the opportunity since they were young and just being groomed.

The women and girls of the community were full of joy. One of them said, "*I knew these were not ordinary boys. They have some good spirits in them.*" No sooner had she said it, the others came in veneration of the two. The boys didn't know how to respond. It was a bit overwhelming for them to witness all this. But they went along with the flow of the situation. Some of the girls were eyeing them and giggling. This made them even more uncomfortable. They blushed and the skin turned reddish. The elders in the community saw all this and laughed.

Then it was time for the preparations for dinner. The hunters all washed themselves after the tough day and conditions they encountered in the woods. The two men who were flung by the boar were tended to. Some herbs were put on their wounds which was of course painful. After this they went into their huts to rest. Then it was time to clean up the implements, spears, bows, arrows and axes. These were all kept in a separate place which was considered sacred by the community. After all, it was a lifeline for them and this was one of those days when the spirits were kind to them.

The boys were all pepped up with the accomplishment. They did not want to rest and volunteered to help out with preparation of the meal. The elders and women were initially reluctant but agreed when they saw that help was required. The preparation of the meat from the boar was the toughest part and this lay with experienced hands. The boys were given the task of cutting fruits and vegetables. Even back in their island, this was a routine and they were comfortable doing. The strain of the hunting became palpable after some time. The Shompen boy asked his friend to take it easy as they had a long way to go. It was important for Tibo not to fall sick.

They began talking with some of the peers, both boys and girls who were helping out too in the chores. Conversation was an issue but the Shompen boy rattled off words with confidence which of course led to some light moments of laughter as it was riddled with some mispronunciations. But that didn't deter him one bit. The audience was in awe of him after the successful hunt. Some interesting snippets came out of the conversation. The children did not go to school despite one being set up not far from their community. It seemed that the elders were not happy and felt that it would make them lose their culture. Moreover, while some of them were eager, it was difficult for them to learn a new language. The boys considered themselves lucky back home since the means of communication was Nicobarese in the school that they attended. Moreover, they were taught something about the islands they lived. Maybe the curriculum wasn't framed properly which led to this dis-interest.

The boys then thought that this would be the best time for them to disseminate the knowledge that they had acquired. With the help of a person who knew Nicobarese, they managed to teach some of their peers about the islands. This was interspersed with their journey snippets. Some of the boys and girls were over awed with all this adventure. They never knew the expanse of their islands and the deep seas that separated them. Some of the stories about the Nicobarese and their way of life interested them. Then when they spoke of the other tribes namely the Jarawas, the Great Andamanese and the Sentinelese, the interest increased. The history was captivating on the region from which their ancestors probably came. It was shocking to know that some of them may have come from a far away land. Crossing the wide ocean was something which even the two boys could not comprehend. One of the boys chipped in saying that he had gone to the South Andamans and met the Jarawas. He went onto explain about the features and their culture. It was not very different from the Onges but yet there were unique aspects. He explained that it was not easy for him to befriend the Jarawas and it happened through one of the peers. The language was the biggest issue but his knowledge of Hindi helped a bit. It seemed that the Jarawas had also come in contact with the outsiders and hence picked up a smattering of Hindi. On the lifestyle aspect he added that it seemed very similar including the paint on their faces. The earing habits were quite similar although there were some differences in music and dance forms. The latter also used drums but the beats were faster and more energetic. The boy had even visited a Jarawa school but found little interest Amongst the community. One aspect that he mentioned was that a road cut through the forests and the Jarawa boys waited there for the passing vehicles to give them some eatables like biscuits. The boy yearned to go back to the settlement just to get a taste of those edibles. It was a different matter that probably those doles were doing more harm than good for the indigenous community.

The topic then came to the other tribes. The boys explained whatever they knew about the Sentinelese, the enigmatic people who inhabited the island of North Sentinel. The children were just stunned that very few people actually knew about them. They were believed to be aggressive driving out all others who tried to approach them. Some of the kids became curious about the tribe but the boys could not answer most questions since they themselves knew very little. The Shompen boy, a celebrity now, told them that the indigenous people did not want to interact with outsiders and wanted to preserve the island as it was. One of the boys said, "*Wish we could also live in an island like that with no one to disturb our lives.*" It was a surprising statement and possibly coming out of the effect of interacting with outsiders. The others were ambivalent about all this. For them the things that came from outside the forests interested them. They talked about the different lifestyle of the people staying outside. The comforts of a sturdier dwelling, the cooked food that they ate and the variety of clothes that they wore.

Soon time passed and it was time for the meal. It was an elaborate one including the meat of the animal that they had just killed. There was the usual dance before the feast. It was a circular formation dance with no instruments to accompany the singing. This was quite different from the music and dance of the Nicobarese and Shompen. The boys took some time to understand the steps and then joined in. It was a rhythmic with a song probably to celebrate the hunt. Both men and women participated and it was a festive occasion as the focus was on the boys. There was a lot of enthusiasm and the tempo increased with time. The community had a lot of stamina since the vigorous movements went on for some time. The boys got tired after the exertion in the forests. They rested for some time.

Finally, the dance stopped and the community then gathered for dinner. It was an elaborate one and the entire group joined in. What the boys noticed clearly was the absence of alcohol unlike what happened back in their communities. There were some local brew which was served in the Nicobarese and Shompen tribes on special occasions. The food was well cooked and tasty. They all had a sumptuous meal. The dancing went on post dinner too and the entire community joined in. The boys were the centre of attraction and they revelled in it. After all it was a new experience for them to be part of another indigenous community celebrations. These interactions also gave them a perspective of the Onges and their way of life. Finally, they all became tired and it was time to rest.

****

CHAPTER XIV

Trip to Rutland

The next day, they woke up a bit late. Too tired after the celebrations the day before. A large boat was about to leave for the Rutland island. It looked a modern vessel made out of strong wood. It had been given by the outsiders to some of the Onges community for their fishing activities. The indigenous people had mastered it and used it to get into deeper waters. There was no doubt that this had helped them fish for new varieties and explore waters which they hadn't done so earlier.

After the ablutions, the two boys quickly rushed to board the vessel. They were given a farewell by the community elders. "*Take good care of yourself. You cannot predict how the other tribes would behave. And avoid outsiders as much as you can.*" These were words of wisdom coming from generations of what was told to them by their forefathers. "*There is a small community of our tribesmen on the island. They will help you out.*" The latter was comforting to the two who embarked on their mission. The vessel had around ten people, all armed with spears, bows and arrows for their catch. What caught the attention was the large net they had. The men explained that this was the mechanism to catch in the deep waters It was a large vessel with adequate space for all of them. The boys became so attuned to a sea faring vessel and it seemed that it was part of their lives. No sooner had they left, the shores were out of sight. The vessel was a powerful one and it skimmed the water at a good speed. When they were in open and deep waters, they stopped the vessel, sighting a shoal moving nearby. Out came the large net from one of the storage places. There were three men dragging it. They sought the help of the boys to open it. It was heavy and it was the first time that the two had seen something like this. There was some edibles attached to the net which was being used as a bait for the unsuspecting fish. During their tryst in the open waters, they had seen some fishermen use something similar by throwing it into the water. The men and the boys managed to drag the net and get it to the edge of the boat. The final lift required some strength as they threw it into the water.

Then the wait began. It was all a matter of patience as the men waited for the shoal to come closer. They could see some confusion in the shoal as some entered the net and thrashed about to get out. The boys slowly understood this fishing technique that they knew little about. Back home, they had seen the use of some leaves and bamboo for making something like this to catch fish. But it was not so strong to be used in the deep waters. The net here was sturdier and they managed to trap a lot of fish. The boys slowly understood the intricacies of fishing in the deep waters. It was about silence and patience. The marine creatures were wary even with the bait and only with the passage of time would they nip it. The sense of the wild made them wary and it finally led to mind games between the prey and the tribesmen.

The catch was good but the difficult part was to get the net out of water. They had to be careful so that the trapped fish did not escape. The men had to synchronise themselves to cover the net from the top to encircle the victims. The boys imbibed all this watching the expert catchers execute their plan. The net was lifted slowly onto the vessel. The two also lent their support when the catch was nearly on the deck. They were shocked to see the size of the catch. It was probably the biggest that they had ever seen. Even the men did not expect the quantum of fish in the net. They were elated and thanked the boys for bringing them luck. The catch was then put in a container. It was not an easy task since many of the fish were still live and jumped around. A few of the lucky ones managed to hit the water and get a new lease of life. The ones in the container were sizeable and this added weight to the vessel. All the men on deck were asked to go to the other end of the boat to ensure overall balance.

With the catch stabilised, the vessel sped towards it destination. On the way, they passed some islands in the distance. The Shompen boy was aware of some of them from the maps. But he knew that many of them were uninhabited. There were many vessels in the open waters and he could see the difference from the Nicobar. The latter had more open waters with very little sighting of boats. Probably it was more pristine than the Andamans and its waters. Both of them wondered as to what was in store for them in these set of islands. They were told by the tribes that the influence of the outsiders was more prominent in these islands.

After the passage of some time, a large island loomed up in the background. The men shouted out that this was Rutland. The treelines were similar but it was evident that this was a large chunk of land. The boys were surprised to see a lot of boats anchored on the shores. It seemed more populated than the other islands that they had visited. The Onges men called out to a fishing vessel which responded and asked them to come in a particular direction. All the men on board knew Hindi and could communicate with the fishing vessel. The necessity had made them learn the language. Both the boys had also picked up some words since they knew the importance of it in their tryst. The large vessel was directed into a particular berth where there were other vessels too. The whole area looked so crowded, almost like a market place. As they neared the shored, the boys understood that this was actually a fish market and all the boats were either coming in or moving out with a catch. The place was also noisy as some people shouted out to the boat to anchor in a particular spot. The vessel was berthed and the men with the boys came on shore.

It was clear that all these people were settlers though the boys could make out a few having very similar features of the Nicobarese. Probably some of them had made their way to this island. Many of the locals were staring at the Onges men and the boys too. It was not often that they saw the tribesmen come with their catch. The dark features were the give away though the boys were still able to blend in the crowd. After a brief moment of staring, it was business as usual with the haggling over fish. The noise and the crowd were a bit disconcerting. For Kayat, it was almost like that hospital he had visited when taking the elder. Cacophony and seeming lack of co-ordination was what hit him. However, the teeming sea of people were actually very business like focussing on getting the best prices for their catch. There was probably a method to this seeming madness. The tribesmen began discussing the price for their fish caught in the deep seas. There was lot of shouting in the process. It seemed that if the main Onge was quite experienced as he too did not buck down. The outsiders were amused at his negotiating skill and could not hide an appreciative laugh. They never expected the tribesman to be good at this. The boys also imbibed what they had seen. The entire catch was thus sold at a good price.

For the tribesmen, the monetary value was not of much use in the Little Andaman. While there were some commercial establishments, not much was purchased from them. The sustenance way of life still made them depend on the produce from the forest or the seas. It was quite similar in the Nicobar chain too for the boys. However, there were many Nicobarese who had integrated well with the settlers. They put the money to good use to purchase products which were generally considered luxury for those living in the woods. The Onges men did not see much use for the money in their island where the community was largely self-sustaining. But with the good amount they got with this catch, they decided to buy some things for the community. Spices for putting in their dishes, sturdier bamboo sticks and leaves for building structures, some utensils, mats for lying on the floor and even some insect repellents. While one may argue that these were considered bare necessities in the modern world, their forefathers never had these when leading a sustainable life in the forests.

The boys also accompanied the men and they went to another market on the island. It was teeming with people, with no indigenous people he could recognise from the facial features. It seemed that this island had none. The stares were visible but soon the people got down to their own business. This was also a round of bargaining and the Onge who was the expert was at the task he was best at. Tempers also soured but he held his nerves and managed to get all that they were looking for. The Shompen boy had picked up some words of Hindi and he too joined in. In some places it was absurd and the mosquito repellent was being sold at almost double the price at which they finally struck to deal. The men congratulated the boy on the achievement. It seemed that the boys were picking up the nuances of life outside the forests quite well. They brought some knives, a fishing net and a bag for the boys knowing fully well that they needed all this to survive the adventure that they were about to encounter ahead.

What was clear to the boys was that business itself lacked ethics and it was about fleecing the other party. They also realised that all the hard work of fishing or agriculture did not provide the type of remuneration that these traders made as middle men. It was all about the game of trying to get the best prices for your produce and the mere labour of growing crops or catching marine life was not the only parameter. It was a whole new world outside the forests and one needed to learn the wiles of The trade to survive. That brief period in the market made the boys learn more than anything else. And to be part of this haggling was all the more enriching for them.

****

CHAPTER XV

Unknown Tribesmen

The men were impressed with the boys who had supported them in all that haggling. Both had learnt the wiles of the outside world and seemed ready for their long journey. As they made their way back to the boat, they chatted on a lot of things. Life in the Little Andamans and Great Nicobar and how it was different. A lot was spoken of the settlers too with most conversations hinged on things not very pleasant. Then in the moment of candour, one of the men revealed a secret. "*There are some tribesmen in the deep forests that no one knows about.*" The boys were stumped but the Shompen boy immediately blurted out, "*Are they the Jangil, also known as the Rutland Jarawas?*" The men were stunned into silence. How could this boy know about this tribe which was considered extinct? The boy could read their lips and said, "*I have studied about them and they were the inhabitants of this island. But the information is that they were extinct.*" The men were amazed at this and just stared at the boy for some time.

After order was restored the conversation hinged on these tribesmen. One of the Onges said, "*Some time back, when one of our boats set foot on this island, one of the Jangils who had come to pick some forest produce approached us hesitantly. He seemed comfortable seeing us given the similarity of our features. It is then that he took us to the settlement deep inside the forest. We were all shocked. They spoke a different language and most communication had to be through signs.*" Tibo then asked, "*How did you then come into close contact with them?*" The man's response was, "*We slowly picked up some words and by the second visit could establish some form of communication. One of us had met the Jarawas earlier and their tongue was quite similar to the Jarawa. They told us about how the colonial masters had taken them hostage and was responsible for finishing their numbers. The Shompen boy was curious, "How did these people survive then.*" Once again the response came, "*This group sensed danger and moved into the interior of the forest. Many years later, some people had come looking for the Jangil's but they managed to hide and did not seek to establish contact. They rarely come out into the ocean for fear of being spotted. It was just by chance that we met the man when our boat landed. For them it was clear that any form of contact would lead to further death and the wiping out of the community itself.*"

The boys were now eager to meet the Jangils. After all, this was a startling discovery. One of the men said, "*You must not mention this to anyone you meet. Else this group may not survive. They are the last vestiges of the indigenous people of this island which is now full of outsiders.*" The boys nodded.

They then took the boys to a small settlement deep in the woods. This was a good hour walk through dense vegetation. The pathway was also not very clear and it seemed to be used very infrequently. Probably to keep away people from venturing in. At a clearing, there was a hut and out came a man, not quite dissimilar in appearance to the Onges. He along with his children greeted the visitors. Pleasantries were exchanged though it was clear that language was still a problem. A mixture of sign language and some words. The men then gave some of the goods they got from the market and some money to the family. Soon the boys learnt that ancestors of this family were living on the island for many years. However, with the coming of colonial rule and the outsiders the entire population had perished due to some disease. What the Onges had told them about these tribesmen turned out to be true. Some of them managed to move to the interiors and survive. There was no documentation by the authorities and hence the place was safe for them. None of the outsiders also ventured into this part of the island. However, they did say that there were some close shaves with people venturing close to the settlement.

The huts were quite different from the ones they had. It was very basic with just a roof for cover. The others came out from the adjacent huts which were made of natural material. The boys were introduced to the family. The man and his family were surprised to see the two children with Mongoloid features and completely tanned. Kayat managed to speak some Onge words for greeting. Though the man did not comprehend, he could understand that it was in Onge. He was surprised and asked, "*Where did you learn all this?*". The boy replied, "*It was in the school back in our island and in the settlement of the Little Andamans. We have come here to look at the other indigenous people. We want your help in getting to the Andaman mainland. Our plan is to first seek the Jarawas and then the Great Andamanese.*" The man was a bit stumped. Firstly at the audacity of the boys to explore these lands. And then he had not heard about the Great Andamanese. For a moment he paused. Then he looked at the men accompanying the boys. They nodded.

His first response was, "*This is a dangerous adventure you are embarking upon. It is not safe. Both the other tribesmen and the outsiders could harm you. You are small boys and it is better to you go back to the families*". One of the Onges chipped in, "*They have come a long way from their homes. It requires a lot of bravery to do what they have done. We could never think of doing this at this age. They are Ambassadors of our spirits.*" The last was the killer statement that swayed the views of the man. He agreed to allow them to stay in the settlement so that they could plan their way ahead. However, he cautioned, "*Don't tell about us to the outsiders. They will come and exploit us.*" These were chilling words and reflected their feelings towards others in the island.

****

CHAPTER XVI

Rutland Jarawas

The boys then planned their future course of action. The first aim was to get a boat to the mainland. Kayat thought about the market where they had haggled for commodities. That seemed the best way forward. The Jangil family would not be of much help since they themselves were hiding from the settlers. Moreover, there were people of Nicobarese origin in the island. Therefore, it would be easier for the two to communicate and navigate their way through.

The tribesmen sat down with the Onges and the boys. A conversation was stuck up mainly through sign languages and some Onge words that one of the Jangil men could understand. It seemed that some of the Onges had settled in this island many years back before they moved to the mainland. It was difficult to understand for the boys but their talk was on events after the last visit by this Onge group. One of the stories was that one of the Jangil boy was almost caught by some people who had seen him from afar. However, he managed to give them the slip and moved to the interiors. There was a fear that an alarm would be raised by the others but that fortunately did not happen. Probably they might not have seen the boy clearly to find that the physical features were different.

Whatever little that the boys could make out or was translated down was a shocking piece of information. There were stories told down from generations that some white coloured men had come with their boats and guns and captured the people in the settlement. Some of these men were taken to other islands. However, the story goes that the greater catastrophe was the diseases that people were inflicted with due to the presence of these outsiders. Many died and families were wiped out. The ancestors of this family somehow sensed the danger and went deep into the forests. The stories mentioned that there were instances when they were nearly sighted but somehow they managed to evade the eyes of the colonial masters and settlers. It was a cat and mouse game but lady luck favoured the indigenous people. They were adept at shifting locations to maintain the secrecy. Even when the Onges landed on this island, they were initially reluctant to establish contact. It was indeed shocking that this settlement had managed to evade the outside world.

What was surprising was that through some of the indigenous people like the Onges and the Nicobarese, this settlement had contact with the outside world too. Sometimes, they got some provisions from the markets of the island but the community was largely self sustaining. Their way of life looked more basic than back in the Car Nicobar. The boys came to know that the source of sustenance was primarily the fruits and vegetables that the community grew. Meat came from the animals around like the monkeys, snakes and even some wild pigs. But with the development around the island, the fauna was under pressure and increasingly the numbers had dwindled. Fishing in the seas was not an option and sometimes the caught some fish in the rivulets and streams. Even the huts were very basic although they had stocked some things like utensils that had been procured from the local market. The clothes that the family wore were scanty although one of the children had worn a T shirt, probably given by someone.

The boys could hardly communicate with the family but the latter were happy to see them. They smiled since the man had probably given the signal that they were friends. Before sitting down for the meal, they went to a nearby rivulet for washing. This seemed to be the source of water for the community as all of them washed themselves in the clear waters. It was cold and refreshing which relaxed them after the arduous journey. The meal was simple with no meat. Probably the family had not caught anything that day. It did not take long to finish it and then they all sat with the Onges and the men of the Jangil family. One of the topic of discussion was how to get the boys to the mainland. The Jangil themselves could not help since they were staying incognito. However, one of them said that he would take the boys to a nearly settlement where one of the Nicobarese would be able to help them. This sounded as a good plan. It seemed that these were highly trusted people and were the only contact of the community with the outside world. Many years back one of the Nicobarese men had strayed into the community and was about to be killed. However, one of the elders intervened and spared him since he was a young boy. He stayed on in the settlement for some days before returning. In this period he was able to communicate with the Jangils and told them about the outside world. He never betrayed their trust and disclosed about them only to the close family. The family kept the secret but helped out the community with some things taken from the market. Some of these included utensils, sea fish and rubber mats; things which the community was seeing for the first time. The Jangils also shared some of their natural mats and fruits with the Nicobarese family and both of them developed a close bond. The women of the family had also come to the community and spent a couple of days with them. Having been privy to the interaction with outsiders, they were even more convinced of the need to preserve the secrecy and did not tell others in their village. Thus the community had managed to evade any interest and preserved their culture, albeit with the occasional exchange of gifts from outside. It was said that the bond was so deep that there was even a marriage proposal between the two families. However, the Nicobarese girl finally decided not to live in the remote forests and it fell through.

All these discussions happened over the lunch served. After the meal, the Onges bid farewell to the community. The boys planned to go later with one of the Jangil men to the nearly settlement. It was an emotional moment for them as the men blessed the boys as they made their way back to the sea. The boys also were drawn into this solemn moment and shed a tear. It was not going to be easy for them given the communication gap. However, the Shompen boy was now confident since he had generally picked up some basic terms. The boys first went around the huts in the settlement. There were around five of them and each was occupied by one family. There were some dogs loitering around and were used for hunting pigs. Some crops were being grown in the vicinity and these were basically some vegetables and fruits. One of the huts was larger and this was where one of the elders were living. All the people were curiously glancing at the boys with the distinct mongoloid features. They noticed that the men and women had some white paint on their faces. The women also wore some trinkets probably given to them by someone. The boys felt elated as they were interacting with a community which the outside world was not privy to.

As was the norm in the other communities too, the boys volunteered and were taken in a hunting expedition for wild pigs. A group of five men went about scouting for the animal. They came to the edge of a rough pathway, seeing which the men retreated. It was clear that they did not want to interact with the outside world. After sometime the noise of a vehicle could be heard. The path was being used by people to traverse a stretch of the woods. The men went in deeper to avoid being noticed. It seemed that such things were common and it was sheer luck that they were yet to be spotted.

The search for the pig was not successful. It seemed that the animals were well aware of the presence of the hunting party and avoided any encounter. However, the group spotted a pack of monkeys. With a well aimed arrow, they managed to bring down an animal perched on the top of the tree. It was a large male and had to be speared. The men were overjoyed. It was a success after a long time and now they would have meat on the table for dinner. As usual, the boys were given credit for bringing in luck for the hunt. There was a victory procession back to the settlement. As soon as they reached the huts, a loud cry was let out by the leading men. The others in the settlement reciprocated. They looked up to the sky to thank the spirits and welcomed the boys who had brought them good luck.

The preparation was simple and the community enjoyed it. It was done over a common fireplace. Little condiments were used and it was the women and the girls who were involved in the cooking. There was some talk about the hunt. With the little words that the Shompen boy could follow, it was clear that the conversation centred around how well the arrow was aimed and hit its mark. One of the men said that pigs were difficult to find with reduction in the forest cover. The remaining ones had been hunted down. Then they came to the conversation about the boys. Firstly, that their coming had invoked the good spirits which had brought them luck in the hunt. Then there was the customary dance. It was around the place where they had prepared the meat. There were no drums like the Onges community. It was one man singing something and then the entire group moving around in circles in a rhythm. It was simple but well co-ordinated. The boys too joined and slowly managed to blend in with the steps. It was not very different from that back home excepting the decibel levels were lower without the percussion. The song and dance went around for half an hour before they all got tired. Even an elderly man had joined in despite the age. It was all about a community bonding. And probably they knew that they were the last vestiges of tribesmen who were believed to have vanished from the face of the islands they once inhabited.

Then the conversation went around to the boys. It was decided that they would be taken the next day to a Nicobarese settlement at the fringes of the forest. One of the men there would be requested to help the boys get to the mainland. There were many vessels plying between Rutland and the mainland and they would decide on the best way for the boys to cross over. With all the efforts of the hunt and the dance, the two slept like a log. They woke up late in the morning. It seemed that the others too were exhausted and had not woken up. The boys went for their morning ablutions and returned all refreshed. The others were slowly waking up in the morning as the light of dawn filtered in. The skies were clear and it was a bit windy as the trees swayed. The chirping of the birds was at its peak as the avians were busy with their activities.

Soon it was time for the folks to go into the woods to gather some fruits. The boys helped out too and they managed to get a sizeable amount of berries from the trees. Some of the men got up to the coconut trees to get the fruit. Then surprisingly they saw a pig family which scampered off as soon as they sighted the party. A surprise since they could not spot anything during the hunt the previous day. After they returned, the entire community sat down for a meal. It was again time for bonding. Then the elder decided that the boys could be taken to the Nicobarese village. They were given some edibles and some trinkets. The boys were overwhelmed by the occasion especially since they had seen an indigenous community which was believed to be extinct. They swore to keep this a secret. All of them wished them luck as they embarked upon the journey with a man. This person was one of the Rutland Jarawa who maintained contact with the outside world for the community. It was a long trek through the dense forests. There was no specific pathway created, else it would attract outsiders. It was important to maintain secrecy and even the Nicobarese in the fringe village understood it. On the way, there was an eerie silence and even the chirping of birds seemed to have stopped. It was getting hot and probably they had taken shelter in the thick foliage. The man knew the way well despite no markers. He was the link between the Jangils and the village that they were about to reach. In this errand too, he would take some fruits for the Nicobarese and they would give him something in return. On this journey, the plan was to get some utensils that the community needed. They soon reached the banks of a stream and the three made their way upstream. The water was gushing and was clear. They washed themselves and then made their way. The forests were still thick and it was not easy to walk over the cobbled stones. The noise of the birds came back from the woods since there was a water source for them.

Soon they reached a clearing and out cropped some semi-permanent structures along the banks. They were well hidden amidst the foliage. The man whistled twice and out came a Nicobarese man. He was surprised to see Tibo whom he recognised as one of his kin. Then he looked at the Shompen boy and said, "*Are you a Shompen?*". It seemed he had interacted with the tribe. The Onges men explained the context and how the boys needed his help to cross to the mainland. The Nicobarese man showed an expression of awe and spoke to the boys. It was refreshing to speak to strangers who were fluent in the language. They told him some parts of their story. The man was amazed and seemed to be overawed by the adventure bug of the boys. The fact that the boys came from so far away aroused his curiosity. He took them to his hut. The man was well clothed just like the other Nicobarese who had deeper level of integration with mainstream society. He told them that while he could have lived in the town, the forests attracted him on account of their pristine nature. He stayed with his family in the bucolic surroundings. Very similar to the story of Tibo and his community. Occasionally he would go to the town to get some essentials.

The first part was to exchange gifts with the Jangil. The man spoke the language of the tribe and the two struck up a conversation. In exchange for fruits, the man had some utensils which he parted with. "*I will get my utensils later from the town market*", he said. "*Come, let us have something to eat. You must be hungry after the journey.*" The man laid out an elaborate menu. For the men, it was a quite different from the simple course that they were used to in their island. The Nicobarese family had proper arrangements for cooking and even had electricity available. It was clear that he did not depend on the forest produce and was getting his provisions from outside. In a way, it was a hybrid life that blended mother nature and modernity well. But yet he chose the tougher life in the woods rather than going to any of the urban settlements on the fringes of these forests.

When he heard about the boy's plan, it was an instant connect. "*I would have come with you on this noble cause but I have a family here. But I will help you get to the mainland. There is a fishing vessel going tomorrow and they are my friends. The man it seems had read about the various indigenous people of the islands and was interested in the topic. I would advise you to meet the Jarawas and the Great Andamanese in your sojourn. Avoid the Sentinelese since it can be life threatening*". Those last words probably aroused a greater curiosity in the boys rather than deterring them. After, all they had undertaken a perilous journey fraught with a lot of risks.

****

CHAPTER XVII

Journey to the Mainland

The Jangil man exchanged some gifts with the man and then left for his settlement. He wished the boys well for their journey. The latter thanked him for all the help and promised to come back sometime. However, with all the uncertainties in the journey, it was only a speculation. The Andamanese man then introduced his family to the boys. There was his wife and two small children. The kids were looking curiously at the two. It took them some time to get used to their presence. The boys shared some fruits which the Jangil had given. The children stared at it and then took a bite each. They liked it and gave a smile.

The boys slept in the semi-permanent structure that the man had built himself. It was a far cry from the basic dwellings that the boys were used to. It had luxuries like a bed, utensils, water stored in tanks, grocery provisions etc and yet it was forests all around. The boys had a good sleep in this relative luxury.

They woke up early morning to the chirping of the birds as the light filtered through the thick growth of the forests around. The water supply through a tap was something new for the boys and they did not have to go out to the stream to wash themselves. Soon, it was time for the preparation of the meal. The boys lent a hand to the family with the preparations cooked over a stove that the man had. It was basically a pancake, the type of which the boys had last eaten at the school they went in the Great Nicobar. They were hungry and ate well as the family watched the boys with interest.

Then the man said, "*Now it is time for us to leave for the town. I will introduce you to my friend who is taking a fishing vessel to the mainland.*" They bid goodbye to the wife and the two children. They gave some more fruits to them as a parting gift. The walk was not very long and within a few minutes the forest cover had given way to an open clearing. There were a number of dwellings and it seemed that all the woods had been cleared for settlements. The family was living at the edge of the forests. There was a road too and vehicles were plying. The Shompen boy felt like the hospital journey he had undertaken when taking the elderly man. There were some roadside stalls where people were eating. The Nicobarese man looked quite used to all this and blended well. For the two boys, this was a far cry from the forests that they lived. Tibo had however seen many of his relatives who had integrated with the settlers and dwelt in such an urban environment.

While walking along the road, they soon reached a settlement. They went to one of the houses and called for a man. He came out and was surprised to see his friend with the two boys. "*It has been a long time. Who are these boys?*" They exchanged some pleasantries and then the man told about the story of the two. The person who was also of Nicobarese origin was surprised as all others on the sheer audacity of the boys to undertake this perilous adventure. "*I heard you are going to the mainland. Please take them along.*"

The man immediately agreed. Moreover, he needed some help for the fishing catch and unloading of it in the mainland market. He told the boys about the work they would be asked to do and both agreed. After all, their aim was to get to the mainland. All four of them went to the market and the man in the forest began shopping for some essentials to be taken back. He came to this place on a monthly basis to replenish his stocks. Rooted in the forests but yet not completely oblivious of the urban life outside.

The conversation centred around life in the Rutland. The man referred to the Jangils saying that the indigenous people became extinct due to the loss of their habitat. He seemed well aware of the history of the islands. He mentioned about the settlements in the island and how it had completely transformed the culture of the place and even led to deforestation. There was little to suggest in the conversation that he knew about the Jangil community still surviving deep in the forests. Even his friend seemed to have held back the information about the tribal family. It was probably the best way to ensure their survival and especially their way of life.

Then he said that his fishing vessel would be going to the mainland of South Andaman and the boys had to accompany him immediately. The two washed themselves in the house and were ready. They had to carry some provisions as the man carried his fishing net. It was one of those plastic nets which the two had seen earlier. It was effective in the high seas for trapping large shoals. The provisions were largely some eatables and water to drink. Some of these were packed in plastic covers, ostensibly taken from the grocery stores. The walk to the shore where the vessel was berthed was around 15 minutes. The boat was lying on its side and had to be lifted up. There was another man and the four had to use all their might to put the vessel up. It was then about pushing it into the sea. This also required some effort since it was low tide. There were other vessels around too but most were already at sea. Once they hit the deep waters, the sailing was smooth. The wind was blowing in the right direction as they made their way into the mainland. The modus operandi was the same as the earlier journey. Catch fish in the high seas and then go to the market in the destination for selling these. The fresher the catch, higher the prices.

The boys had garnered adequate experience in high sea fishing. As soon as they hit the blue waters, the first sign was to look at the movement of any birds. They all swooped around spots where there were large shoals. Then one could look at the other fishing vessels in the vicinity. The too focussed on such waters where the probability of a catch was larger. However, today, there were sightings of neither birds or other vessels since they were in open waters. So it was all about visual sight. The Shompen boy then sighted a school of dolphins moving at a frenetic pace. He could see them chasing something and it was obvious that it was a school of fish. He signalled to the two men and they moved closer to the spot of sighting. The hunch was true and there were large shoals of fish. They immediately unveiled the net and threw it into the waters. Lady luck smiled on them as a large shoal of fish unsuspectingly jumped into the net. The men were also surprised since they had not seen such a catch. They had never followed the path of dolphins since this patch of sea was always full of catch. But today the boys, albeit with their limited experience, had taught them a new trick.

They dragged the heavy net onto the vessel. It was a stunning catch and all four of them were tired by the time they got in on board. The two men gave out a victory cry. It was one of those surreptious days. Then it was time for the vessel to be taken to the mainland. They soon sighted some vessels in the water. Within an hour, treelines came into view. The place was crowded with boats and the men manoeuvred their boat to a place on the banks. it was a point of disembarkation and there was a rope attached to a pole. No sooner did they touch shore than the two men jumped out and tethered the vessel. The entire shore looked crowded as it was teeming with people. It looked like a market place where people were selling their wares. But for the boys, it was a relief. They had reached the Andamans mainland, which was a major objective. Things had been rosy till now but the real challenge began here. How would the Jarawas, Great Andamanese and the Sentinelese react to them?

****

CHAPTER XVIII

Pathway to the forests

On shore, the four offloaded their catch. Some of the other fishermen were looking at the catch with envy. They were even more surprised to see the two Nicobarese and the two boys on the vessel. It seemed that most of the fishermen were locals and it was rare to find the indigenous people in this trade. They set up a stall in a vacant space nearby.

Soon the place was thronged by potential buyers. One of the men did the first trade and the two boys could clearly gauge that he was fleeced since he agreed to the price quoted. So they spoke to the men who seemed novices. The boys had after all picked up some nuances from their experience in their long journey. The men agreed to the boys negotiating the rates. The Shompen boy was put in charge due to his familiarity with the language. Another person came with the same quote as the last transaction. Word had spread in the market that the group of four would sell their wares dirt cheap quite out of the market rates.

But the Shompen boy stuck to his guns. "*This is not the right price. You will have to double the rates.*" He had heard the rate for the transactions in the adjacent stalls and started with even a higher quote. The two men were surprised and felt that no one would take from them. The buyer let out a laugh. "*You have no idea of anything. No one would buy your fish and you would need to return empty handed.*" He moved away. One of the Nicobarese told his friend. "*I told you these boys don't understand the business. He is too young for all this.*" The boy motioned to the men to keep quiet. "*Just wait and watch. They are just playacting.*" It was a typical cat and mouse game. The potential buyer had signalled to the others that these men were asking too much. So others kept out. The absence of customers was peeving the men more than the two boys. They were impatient and wanted to sell their produce and move back to Rutland. The boys calmed them down. "*What is the use of not getting enough money for your catch? This has been one of our lucky days and we should get just reward for it.*" The men were not happy but they went along with the boys.

No sooner had time passed and the frustration of the men was getting palpable than one old man came. He surveyed the fish and said, "*This is the freshest lot that I have seen in this market. When did you catch it?*" The men were just thinking about responding when Tibo chipped in, "*It is just an hour and we got it from the deepest part of the sea.*" While the time may have been off the mark, the part of the depth was not incorrect. Even Kayat was surprised at the fast response which was not entirely right. Even his friend had learnt a lot in their tryst. The man surveyed the fish again as if to check the veracity of what was told to him. He then quoted a price much higher than the first transaction but not exactly double of it. Immediately the Shompen boy chipped in, "*We can agree if you raise it by another ten rupees.*" The men were a bit embarrassed by all this and did know how to respond. The buyer was also taken aback by the boy's response. He surveyed the boy, then the catch and finally agreed to the price. The two men were in a state of shock. They had visited this market so many times but today the two boys had taught them a lesson in bargaining.

As soon as the old man bought the fish and was helped by the boys to take it an assigned place, other buyers came in. There was something that attracted them to this place. The boys understood that probably their catch was the freshest among the lot available. Even the man who had mocked them came back. His first question was, "*Have these boys come from some large town? They are very smart.*" This was a complement coming from someone who had laughed at them some time back to pressurise them. But the man was playing mind games and could not hold his patience for long. The more the time, the freshness of the fish would have gone and the four had the best catch in the market. He would sell this fish at a much higher rate than that though his expected profits would wane.

Soon the catch was sold and the men were very happy. They immediately rushed to the market to buy some provisions. There was a larger variety than what they got in the island and it was cheaper. They brought some edibles for the boys and parted with some money too. They then took them to a place where one of their friend emerged. The man was surprised to hear about the amount of money they had got in the market for the catch in the deep waters. He was a Nicobarese too and they told him about the boy's plan. The man was taken aback but promised to help. He was surprised that Tibo and his family still lived in the forests since most of the Nicobarese had integrated with the outside world. He was seeing a Shompen for the first time and was curious about Kayat. Kayat was confident enough to narrate the reason of their rendezvous. He even talked about how they would like to meet the Jarawas first and then try to reach out to the Great Andamanese. The man was surprised at the boy's confidence and clear thought process.

The boys first bid farewell to their hosts in Rutland. It was another emotional one as there was a deep connect. Probably the fish catch and the haggling in the market had made that bond strong. What was clear was that the boys had learnt the tricks of life outside the forests but this was the essence of survival in this part of the world. They went back to the house of the host to discuss the plan. It was not going to be easy to go the Jarawa settlement as they were considered aggressive. The communication problem would exacerbate the issue and one could never predict the type of response.

The Shompen boy suggested that it they were left in the fringes of the woods where the Jarawas stayed, the two would move ahead. But the man did not agree to this since it was risky and given their different features, there was a likely chance of the tribe attacking them with arrows. Even Tibo was not in favour of the two trying something on their own. But slowly the realisation dawned that only designated officials of the administration interacted with the tribe. The latter was unlikely to help out the two boys from the Nicobar chain to interact with the Jarawas. There was already a lot of suspicion since the outside interaction with the tribe had led to some unsavoury incidents. Hence, it was the two on their own. The man then said, "*I will leave you at the fringes of the forest. You would need to make your way from there.*"

The man was planning to cross the forest where the Jarawas lived. But then he could not drop the boys in the middle since it was a convoy that went. A better option was to drop them on the outskirts when all the vehicles stopped to get their passes. No one would notice if the boys surreptiously went off into the woods. He hired a vehicle and the two boys got in. The driver did not suspect despite the Shompen boy having distinct features. It was the first time that the boys saws real urbanisation. There were some big houses, large crowds coupled with run down shops and green forest cover. It seemed they all co-existed. Kayat had similar feelings as the drive with the elder who was taken to a hospital. There was chaos though there was an order to all this. For Tibo, it was a bit of a shocker as he had not witnessed such a frenetic activity. It was only when the vehicle passed a forest cover that he got back his nerves. It was clear that he had not strayed much beyond the woods excepting for probably the school.

Anyhow the drive was long and it took them a good two hours to reach the destination. They all got down for some refreshments. They had what looked like a rice cake dipped in a curry. The two were having this for the first time. They then gulped down a glass of water. It gave them the much needed energy. The man then took them inside the woods. He traversed it as if he knew the topography well. He then said, "*I had also tried to reach out to the Jarawas through this route without telling anyone. A daring adventure like you two are attempting. But then after a long walk, I saw a group with their arrows. It was scary since I had heard about them killing outsiders. I hid and retreated.*" Rather than being scared, the boys were more curious. Tibo said, "*Maybe you should have just called out to them. They would not have sensed any threat and shot any arrow. The arrows were meant for the prey they were scouting.*" The man laughed, "*Let me see your reaction when you come across them.*"

They then reached a spot and the man said. "*Do you see this path. It has been made by some Jarawas who wanted to come and see the outside world. Some of them still use it. So be careful. Best of luck to you too. I can only wish that something untoward doesn't happen. I have to rush back since the vehicles would be leaving for the forests.*"

With that the boys were on their own. Their destiny was in their hands.

****

CHAPTER XIX

The Jarawa Encounter

The boys rested for some time to take stock of the situation. It was time for them to summon all the courage for the journey ahead. There was no doubt that this was going to be their toughest test yet as the tribesmen had an unpredictable behaviour. Anyhow the boys trudged ahead. They exercised the utmost caution trying to keep on the side of the pathway to avoid detection. Their ears were glued for any sounds just like they did during their hunting expeditions. But the Jarawas were known to be skilful hunters with keen senses. They did not want to fall into a trap.

The journey was long and the boys had penetrated deep into the forests. The growth was heavy and even the path became very narrow. They wondered if they were on the right way. Suddenly, the Shompen boy heard some noises. He paused and the two went into the woods to check. The noises seemed to come closer and the boys were filled with trepidation. Then they stopped and the boys looked in that direction. As if some faces would suddenly peep out of the woods to confront them. They just froze to be prepared for the worst. Strangely the noises stopped. The boys were certain that this was a group of tribesmen in the vicinity. The Shompen boy even wondered if they had spotted the two and were just hiding to catch them offguard.

But with the silence, it was clear that whoever was making those noises had moved away. But the boys were still not sure and had to be cautious. But to their surprise, they suddenly heard the noises of some vehicles and lo behold it was a road in front of them. There was a loud roar of a number of these vehicles. It seemed like a full convoy was passing. It was kicking dust as they made their way. The boys hid since they did not want to give away their position. They waited for the vehicles to pass through and saw them from a vantage point. It included cars, trucks, buses and even two wheelers. The dust settled and they had to decide the path to be taken.

Then suddenly out of nowhere a few children emerged. These were clearly the Jarawas and wore scanty clothing. The two were well hidden and were unsure about what to do. One thing was certain that the children would not attack them but then there could be grown ups alongside. Seeing the boys in the presence of their children could potentially lead to violent reactions. The two friends looked at each other and the expressions suggested that they remain hidden. The Shompen boy whispered, "*Let us wait for some adults. Maybe they would see us as a lesser threat without their children around.*" They agreed and decided to tail the children. It was difficult to catch the youngsters since they were well versed with the terrain and sped into the dense cover. The boys managed to keep up with them for some time. The plan was that they would take them to their settlements.

No sooner did they manage to catch up with the children than an arrow came flying in the direction of Tibo. It narrowly missed him and landed in the trunk of a tree. The two ran with all the energy they had. It was a close shave and any mortal would have frozen. But the two scurried deeper into the forests. It seemed that someone had seen them tailing the children and came after them. But he could still be close by and this forced the two to continue with their frenetic pace. They were literally out of breadth than they could feel another arrow come their way. This was wayward but it forced them to move in the opposite direction. Despite being almost out of breadth, it was time for them to scoot from the place. There was danger all around and they needed to reach a safe haven. It was clear that the first encounter with the Jarawas did not go off well.

The boys stopped only when they were absolutely sure that there was no one following them. With the bagpacks that they were carrying, it was indeed tiring to run through the woods like this. Their life in the forests had helped them come out of this life threatening situation. For anyone living in the urban chaos, they would surely have been caught by the men in bow and arrow. And maybe they would not have been alive to tell the tale. Fortunately for them, they heard the sound of a stream and moved towards that. They soon reached the water body and washed themselves and had a good sip. But they had to be on their guard with the men possibly on their heels. It was certain that this was a matter of life and death for the two. However, it was instinct which told the Shompen boy to move away from the stream into the woods. He pulled Tibo with him and scurried for cover. The latter was surprised since there did not overtly seem to be anything which should have caused any concern. However, the sixth sense was dot on the mark as out came three men with bows and arrows looking around for someone, surely the two boys. They came to the stream and washed themselves but their eyes were looking out for any sign of movement. The three children that they saw on the road also came out and they too were scouting. It was clear to the two boys that the three had probably realised that they were being tailed and informed the men.

The two maintained pin drop silence. The presence of some monkeys also did not deter them. They were focussed on the job at hand to evade. By the looks of it, the three men were definitely not friendly and there was no point of revealing their positions. It would have been fatal. The boys had to bide their time and then look elsewhere. They were not sure if the people of this community were in touch with the other tribesmen in the forests. If the presence of the two boys was being communicated throughout the place, then there was no way that they could approach the others. But they had an objective to fulfil and this was not the time to overcook the thought process. The wait was excruciating since the six of them were surveying the bushes around with that determined look. The boys went in deeper into the woods making as little as noise as possible. The men were yelling in a direction of the noise made by the troop of monkeys. They stopped only when they saw the simians. It was a close shave.

Soon they had to take a break to strategise. This happened again at a stream. They were not sure if it was the same. But after refreshing, they had to quickly get back into the woods. One could never gauge as to when some of the tribesmen could appear. After all a source of water was the best place for them to gather. The boys were now hungry and had to eat something. There were some fruits in the bagpack but they also looked out for any berries. After all they did not want to exhaust their reserves. There were some coconut trees but it was too taxing to climb up and even more risky given that someone could sight them. They plucked some berries from the trees and tasted them. It was something they had seen earlier and the Onges were eating it. Therefore it could not be poisonous. They ate some of the fruits and quenched their thirst.

Then back in the woods, they scouted to see if there was anyone around the stream. Then they decided to make their way deeper into the forests. It was better to avoid the pathway since there could be some Jarawas around. After travelling some distance, they heard some noises. Treading with caution, they reached a clearing where there was a hut. This was clearly a hut of the tribesmen. The Shompen boy whispered, "*Let us wait and watch. We should not startle them since that might lead to some aggression.*" No sooner had he whispered than a woman came out. She peered in their direction since probably she had heard some of their whispers. The boys hit behind some trees and then waited. Tibo had a sixth sense suggesting that the woman might not jump at the sight of the two and could actually be helpful. He was planning to come out of the hiding and reveal himself when Kayat held his hand and said, "*What are you doing? Not now.*"

It seemed that the woman heard it and she said something in a loud tone. Neither of the boys understood the language though the Shompen boy with his sharp perception made out that the woman was asking them to come out. Words however, softly whispered travelled far. It was as if the woods and the winds thereof were a means of transmission of even the softest tones. She moved swiftly in their direction and the boys were momentarily indecisive. Then she called to one of her children, a boy who came out and also went in the direction where the boys hid. Tibo told his friend, "*I am sure she will help us out. I can judge people by their tone.*" The Shompen boy was not convinced but he had no choice. Both of them were closely at their heels and it was only a matter of time that they were caught.

So the boys called back. The two caught up with them. The child was a bit stunned to see the two boys who had different physical features from their kinsmen. The woman however seemed less surprised. She had probably interacted with either the Nicobarese or the Shompens. She spoke something which the two didn't understand. Then she spoke in Hindi which both the boys could comprehend. They too were surprised that the woman dealt with the entire situation very calmly. She said, "*Where are you two coming from? Why do you want to put your life in danger? They may attack you with arrows which could be fatal.*" The boys were well versed with this situation and just needed to parrot their story which they often told the others. But this time they were more circumspect. Somehow the woman inspired a lot of confidence and they said, "*We have already been chased by some of your kinsmen since we were not sure as to how to interact with them. Our journey is only to find out about the indigenous people of our islands such as the Jarawas. We come in peace and would soon leave to find the other indigenous people of the land. You have to help us reach your elders and explain to them that we do not intend to create any problems. We have already seen the Onges and the Jangils.*"

The woman also seemed to trust the two and first took time to comprehend what they had said. She responded, "*You must be wondering as to how I speak Hindi? I have also stayed outside the forests but decided to come back to the lives in the forests. We have had some skirmishes with the outsiders but now the situation is better. They take good care of our medical issues and even give us some food from the towns. As for the men who you confronted, I will speak to our elders but you two stay in hiding till that.*" She then asked them to come close to their settlement since she wanted to give the boys something.

Despite the calm demeanour, the boys did harbour some suspicion. They had read about the dangerous encounters with the Jarawas. There were even instances of death as they attacked the outsiders. They had also learnt about the attacks on the workers making the road running through the forest. They however, reluctantly followed the woman to the settlement. She asked them to stay at a particular spot. Both she and the child went inside the settlement and soon came out with another child. They were carrying some fruits for the boys. "*Here, keep them with you. You might feel hungry if it takes a long time. Both of you also look tired.*" Whatever misgivings they may have had of her simply vanished. She seemed to be a good hearted person who wanted to help the two. And she was buying into their story about the adventure they set out on. More importantly, they had told her the correct picture of the encounter with the Jarawas and she would know how to handle the tricky situation in case information filtered about the two boys who had trespassed into the tribe's territory.

They waited and bid their time. Of course after refreshing themselves with the fruits given. It was a cat and mouse game. The woman was speaking to someone inside the hut. Then after sometime, out came a man. The woman motioned the boys to come out. They did not know how to react to the man. He was glaring at them with bloodshot eyes, a frightening proposition for the youngsters. Finally, the man said, "*Are you telling the true story? Why did you run away from the men of our tribe? How do you propose to go to the places you want to?*" The boys responded that they were not sure of the intention of the men since they were armed with bows and arrows. On their plan, they just said that they had managed to come all the way to the mainland without any harm. And the spirits would take care of them.

The man surveyed the two. He checked their bagpacks to see if there were any spears, bows or arrows inside. When convinced that the boys were just harmless, he called up the others. Soon a group of men, women and children from the Jarawa settlement came out. They all were staring at the two as if they were some museum artifacts. Some of the children came close and even touched the boys. Curious as to why their colour was different from theirs. The two felt a bit uncomfortable but they did not want to offend their hosts. After all they had broken the ice and this was a key achievement for them in their journey. They just smiled. The Shompen boy knew some basic words and blurted those out. The children were amused and they reciprocated with words and smiles. The boys could make out that the tribes were dark complexioned and some of them had the same red and white paint that the Onges put on. They were all bare bodied and the paint was all over the bodies too. The women and the girls wore some ornaments. The entire community got together and surveyed them.

The man and the woman who had initially spoken as well as an elder seemed to be the only one who knew the language of the outsiders. The elder had the same questions to the boys as some of the others, "*Why did you undertake this perilous journey? You could get killed since many feel threatened by outsiders. I have heard about your community in the Nicobar. I am amazed that you could come all the way to this place unharmed.*" These were comforting words for the boys and they repeated their answers that were given to the others.

Soon the peers of their age came out and they were giving a cold stare. The boys felt a bit uncomfortable as some of them even touched them. The elders shooed the children who were coming too close to them. Even the girls of the clan came close but they showed some signs of shyness. It was awkward to say the least for the two as this went on for some time. But the boys had that inner happiness that they had cracked this tough part of their journey. The Jarawas were told to be very unpredictable but this group seemed friendlier. The boys went with the flow of the moment.

Then one of the elders said something to his kinsmen. The Shompen boy could barely understand but it seemed more of a scolding for them to get his people back to where they came. Then he told the boys, "*Come we will show you around out place*". He and a few other men then took the boys around the settlement. There were a few huts, very similar to the ones of the Onges. It was made of bamboo and some other materials. The boys noticed that while they were bare chested, the trunks were covered with some skirts made of forest materials. The dark coloured skin were painted in red and white clay. Nearly everyone had their bodies with these markings. Not very dissimilar to what they had seen elsewhere. It was mutual curiosity as the families were also looking at the boys with Mongoloid features. Probably, they had not seen people of such origin. The boys noticed that the houses were well adorned with some things that seemed to have come from outside the forests. They later came to know that some of these were gifts given by passing vehicles on the main road that cut through the forests where they lived.

Then one of the men who understood the language conversed with them. He told them about the interaction of the tribes with the colonial rulers and now the settlers outside the forests. From the tone, it was obvious that these interactions did not go as intended. He said, "*Many of the outsiders are friendly and give us gifts. But then there are some who take advantage of us and mock us. Basically, our way of life and the fact that we are scantily clad unlike them. Our dark complexions are also a measure of the curiosity. But the forest cover around is diminishing as the settlements are hungry for land. It is a conflict that we are living with.*" The man was very articulate and seemed very knowledgeable about the circumstances surrounding the interface between the indigenous people and the outsiders. He seemed to have understood the thought process of the two and then said, "*There are many well intentioned people who want to help us and sustain our way of life. But then there are circumstances that they cave into the pressures of the denudation of the forests. After all their way of life is so different from ours.*"

The boys sat down and offered to join in any hunting or food gathering expedition. The man immediately agreed to and asked them to accompany some of the children who were going to gather some fruits and nuts from the nearby forests. There were four children and the six decided to go ahead. The task was to get some coconuts and jackfruits. One of the bigger boys looked like the leader and he led the way. He said something to the boys which the Shompen boy translated to mean that they would cross a road. This was the road that the boys had heard about. It was said to cut through the forests that the Jarawas inhabited and was used as a means of transport by the outsiders to travel. They were all excited to see for themselves. The vegetation was dense as the boys made their way. There was a time when it seemed the group lost the way but the leader soon got them back on track.

Then suddenly there was a rumbling sound. Sounded much like thunder but the sky was clear. The children were excited and they all ran towards it. The boys were surprised and initially were reluctant to follow the group. Life in the forests had taught them to be circumspect of any sound. Here this motley group had thrown all caution to the winds and was ironically moving in the direction. The sounds came closer and there was honking too. It was then that it dawned on the two that these were vehicles on a road. But the sound seemed to suggest that there would have been many vehicles. Soon there was a cloud of dust kicking up as they neared the convoy of vehicles. The dust came directly in the direction of the group blinding their vision of sight. It was like a yellow mass approaching them. It irritated the two but the Jarawas boys seemed used to this. They rushed into this cloud and motioned for the two to follow. Once they entered that zone, there was no visibility but the sounds grew louder. Finally, they all climbed and reached the road. It was a perfect co-ordination as they saw the front end with the first vehicle letting out a siren. It had some blinking lights and it made a shrieking noise. This was ostensibly to warn the tribe and avoid any accidents.

The boys had already seen a convoy and this one too had cars, buses, transport vehicles and even two wheelers. Most of the occupants of the cars and buses looked intently at the boys. They were pointing fingers and looking at them with amazement. The tribal boys seemed used to such attention but the two squirmed a bit. It was a bit uneasy to be peered at, as if they were some specimens in a museum. And ironically the gaze was more on them. Probably since they stood out. One of the vehicles which had a siren stopped and also looked at the two boys. One man got down from the vehicle and came close to the two. Everyone was looking at this drama. Suddenly the four boys gave a signal for all to run. Even the two realised that the person was just inspecting who these boys were in the midst of the Jarawas. In the confusion, they too ran. The man realised the situation and shouted for the others in the vehicle to follow him. They ran after the group. But the six were very adept. The forest was their home and they were experts in weaving their way through the dense undergrowth. The men gave chase for some time but soon realised the futility and gave up. Moreover, they could not hold back the convoy.

The boys got separated from the Jarawas and were on their own. They soon managed to find one of the boys. For the first time they saw a smile on one of the Jarawa boys. While nothing was said, the expression meant that he felt that the two as part of their community. It was clear to him that the two were also boys of the woods and the settlers had come to displace them. The three of them made their way to the settlement. But not after gathering some fruits and nuts, the mission on which they were sent. As soon as they reached the huts, the boy told the men about the incident. One of the other boys in the group which had reached earlier had already conveyed the message about the incident.

The village got together. They too had the same emotions as that of the Jarawa boy. For them the boys, despite the differences in physical characteristics were part of their way of life. They had embraced them as one of their own. There were hugs. How else could this end but with a feast and dance. The food was sumptuous to say the least. Pork, rice and vegetables. Looked like they had a successful hunt the previous day. The dance was full of vigour with the beating of drums and a fast-paced rhythm. And how could the boys not join in. Some of the Jarawas were laughing at the boy's inability to match some of the steps but then the two soon matched these and enjoyed themselves to the hilt. It went on late into the evening and only stopped when the stamina had given way. The two felt themselves to be part of the community.

For the boys, this was a one of the difficult parts of their journey. They had come out with flying colours. They clearly felt that the perception that the outsiders had of the tribe being aggressive and unfriendly was misplaced. They had a different way of life which the others could never understand. And the encounters with the colonial powers who came and those who ruled had etched a painful stigma on the psyche of the indigenous people. This had probably carried down the generations and each step forward was being taken with a lot of trepidation. And no wonder, they were cautious and sometimes aggressive to preserve their culture.

****

CHAPTER XX

Escape in the Andaman forests

The boys had to decide their future course of action. It was not safe to stay here since word would have disseminated to the powers that be about their presence in the Jarawa settlement. It would create problems for the tribe since they would be questioned. Hence, they had to make their way out.

No sooner did this thought process filter through that one of the Jarawa men told them, "*You have been spotted by the outsiders and they will come looking for you. So it is better that you try to go deeper into the forests or further up along the coasts. You could meet some other tribesmen of ours or maybe even the Great Andamanese.*" The two were surprised that the man knew about the other tribesmen which the boys were thinking of encountering. He had probably come in touch with the outside world and had a good inkling about the indigenous people of the islands. It also signalled the fact that the elders had congregated and decided that the boys presence could create trouble for them as others would come looking for them.

The boys gathered their wits and decided to leave the place. However, instead of going away from the settlement, they concurred on going to some distance away and keep a vigil to see whether anyone came looking for the two. That night, they moved away to some distance in the forests. It was not difficult for them to survive the night since they had a good experience trudging in the wild undergrowth in the Nicobar and these forests looked nearly the same. If not less dense.

The night was silent. It was only broken by the chatter of a monkey troupe nearby. The simians had probably been scared by an animal and were warning their breathen. It seemed unlikely that they were affected by the presence of the boys. However, there were some ants crawling on the ground and this was a source of uneasiness for the boys who decided to then perch themselves on a low tree. The swaying of the branches ensured that they did not get enough sleep as the first light of dawn hit. The birds were out with their chirping and the troupe of monkeys nearby spotted them. They quickly scattered since they were afraid of being hunted. Not surprising given the practise of the Jarawas. The boys washed themselves in a nearby stream and were on the lookout for anyone coming. No sooner had they managed to eat some berries from the nearby trees, they heard the clutter of boots nearby. From their place of hiding, they could make out around five outsiders going towards the Jarawa settlement. The men had a bagpack each and they wore heavy boots. It was obvious that they were not used to the rough terrain.

So the hunch was correct. The men would come looking for the boys. And they would question the elder men. It was time for them to scoot before any trouble befell the tribesmen. They tiptoed for some time to prevent any sound percolating. Then once they had created some distance, they walked briskly. It was in the direction of the road. The path cut through the forests of the Jarawas and would take them further north. In the direction of the Great Andamanese, the next set of indigenous people that the boys wanted to meet. But the task was not going to be easy. The road would have the flow of vehicles and they could be caught. And once the forests ended it would be filled with settlements. It was not going to be easy to traverse without arousing suspicion.

After some travel, they reached the road. It was deserted but the boys knew that at any time a convoy could pass. It was better to be at a safe distance. However, once a convoy went past, they could risk coming to the road for a brisker pace. But it did carry the risk of another convoy coming from the opposite direction. The strategy worked well and they made good distance. When a convoy came up, they quickly scurried to the undercover and kept out of sight. When it was safe enough, they decided to hit the road again. It was a classic cat and mouse game but the progress was creditable. Unlike travelling in the forests when the undergrowth and the attendant risks like snakes could considerably slow down the pace. Once they reached the edge of the forests which had a guard post, it was getting dark. So they decided to take rest. Fortunately, they found a shelter in the guard room. It was deserted as they cautiously entered and surveyed it. There was a bed with even some water bottles left. This however aroused their suspicion with a better option of maintaining a safe distance and enter late in the night when they were certain.

This is precisely what they did. Prior to that they had a hearty dinner which they had carried from the Jarawa village. It was washed down with some water from a nearby stream. They came across a group of Jarawas too but avoided them since they were not sure about the response. Especially when there were others tailing them and probably questioning the tribesmen. Finally, once the coast was clear, they slept in the guard room. In the middle of the night, they heard some noises and came out in a hurry. But it was just a family of pigs scurrying along the road. The boys woke up as the dawn cracked. They needed to move out since the settlers could be nearby and a convoy would also be moving. They refreshed themselves and had a light snack which they carried. Now came the difficult part of moving out of the forests without being caught by any of the enforcement authorities. So they decided to wear some clothes they had and merge with the settlers population. They could easily pass off as Nicobarese, many of who had joined the mainstream society. When the coast was clear, they came out of the forests. Some spotted them but no one suspected. Two boys, looking very much like settlers were now free birds for their next destination.

****

CHAPTER XXI

Preparations for the encounter

They now had to strategise for the next rendezvous. On land, it was easier to get some transport but then the crossover to the island would be the challenging part. They managed to blend well and passed off as Nicobarese. They first stocked themselves with some provisions at the market. In the journey through the forests, they had run out of food and water. Then it was the ferry to the large island of Baratang. Some people stared at Kayat but he managed to converse with enough confidence to confuse them. After all, he could speak both Hindi and Andamanese. The ferry journey was a short one as they managed to intermingle with the hordes of tourists who were going to the island.

Once they docked at the island, they refreshed themselves. It was now time for them to take up some more provisions. Then the walk on foot along the main road of the island began. It moved along in the northern direction of the island. It would further lead to the Middle Andamans. The boys had studied the route in their school and knew the point on the road wherein they had to take a detour. They managed to reach this point by the afternoon as the sun was beating down on them. From here onwards, it would be a trek through the forests till the north eastern edge of the island. They sought directions and some of the people were surprised at the two boys going in that direction. The forests were dense but there were some open spaces which suggested either habitation or the route being used by others. This facilitated a faster progress thought the undergrowth. The boys were anyhow adept in this sort of terrain. They had grown up in an area which was tougher than this to traverse. It was only the direction which was an issue. But with the type of habitation the island had, it was unlikely that they would get lost. As luck would have it, they came across a pathway. They followed it and it soon hit the shores.

Now they had to get information on how to get to the Strait island. The island was not very far but it was restricted since the Great Andamanese inhabited it. It was a protected reserve and not many means of transport were available. The boys enquired from the locals. Some of them were suspicious while others provided some vague information. Finally, they met a Nicobarese man who took the boys to his home. He had read about the

Shompens and asked Kayat as to how he landed up here. The boys had to tell their story. The man's worry was not about the next trip but the last leg of the journey. "*Why are you taking such a big risk? The Sentinelese will not spare you? They are known to kill anyone in their vicinity.*" The boys ducked the question since they did not want to think that far. Tibo said, "*Our first aim is to reach the Great Andamanese. We need to meet them and understand them better. After that we will see what fate has in store for us.*" The man was impressed at the maturity of the boy. He asked Tibo, "*I see you are not well. What is the matter?*" The Shompen boy chipped in. "*We do not know. Even our medicine man and the hospitals of the settlers have not been able to get to the root of it. My friend develops high fever on and off. Sometimes he gets very tired while at other times he is normal.*"

The man was surprised. "*This is a serious matter and you boys still want to do this journey. You may pass on some of your ailments to the tribes that you are visiting. Are you aware that so many of them died because of the diseases transmitted by outsiders. Many of these tribes cannot even survive a small cold.*" The boys were surprised at the man's knowledge but the Shompen boy responded, "*We are also people of the forests and have not interacted with the settlers. This is our first journey and we do not carry any of the dangerous diseases that you are imagining. We will not be a threat to them. By the way, how do you know all this?*" The man revealed that he was involved in the study of the tribes, chiefly the Great Andamanese. He used the term "*anthropologist*" for the first time and explained to the boys about what his work was. However, he confessed that he was yet to visit the Sentinel Island though it was one of his desires. "*You see the government has stopped contacts with them. They do not want the tribe to be disturbed with outside influences. They even survived the tsunami that hit the island. It is important to preserve their culture.*" The man was a treasure trove of information for the boys. And to top it all, he had visited the Great Andamanese, the next stop for the boys too.

He provided information on the tribe. "*They are suspicious of outsiders since they were once the dominant tribe of the main island. The colonial rule and other outsiders marginalised them and today they are confined only to the Strait Island with around fifty of them left. But they are also slowly losing their culture and with the facilities provided by the government, they have undergone a transformation. Many of their cultural traits have also disappeared and even their language is in danger.*" He then went on to describe the various sub tribes of the settlers that once inhabited the Andaman group of islands starting from the Yerewa subgroup in the North which has further subdivision of tribes like the Kari, Kora, Bo and Jeru. Then there was the Bojigyab or the Southern sub group that comprised of the Kede, Kole, Juwoi, Pucikwar, Bale and Bea. He explained the cultural difference of these subdivisions and how the colonial rule and penal settlements changed the entire dynamics. Moreover, diseases had killed many of them and they are now confined to the Strait Island.

Finally he said what the boys had come for. "*You have come to the right person. I have to visit the tribe for furthering my study. You too can join me in the trip and help me with my work. There would be a surprise in store for you. But we would go only tomorrow.*" The boys could not believe their luck. It was as if fate had ordained for them to achieve their ambition. They only hoped that this fortune would continue especially when they encounter the gravest dangers in the fag end of their trip to the North Sentinel.

The man then asked the boys to come to his dwelling. They gleefully accepted it with a complete trust on what the man had said. After all he was one of the tribe and was studying the Great Andamanese. On the way back, they saw many brick structures as the island was inhabited by the settlers. Strangely when they reached the man's house, it was a near replica of the home that Tibo stayed. The same markings of a forest home of the Nicobarese. It looked strange in the midst of some permanent settlements. It was a sign that the man was passionate about his subject and wanted to replicate the environment that he sought to study. The boys surveyed the hut. It had some modern amenities like water supply from a nearby source and a cupboard but the rest of it was as bare as it could get. Bamboo mats, bare utensils, some natural decorations etc dotted the structure. There was an extra room and the man asked the boys to occupy it. He told them that his family was staying in one of the Nicobar islands, a place which was less influenced by settlers. They then settled down and the man continued with his discourse on the Great Andamanese, those on Strait Island as well as the others who had blended with the mainstream population in the Andamans. It was interesting for the boys and enough fodder for them when they interacted with the Great Andamanese. The food that the man made was also frugal namely vegetables and raw fruits, a far cry from what was available on the island they were currently on. The tone had been set for their journey ahead. And they were looking forward to the surprise that the man mentioned.

****

CHAPTER XXII

Strait Island

They woke up early the next day and refreshed themselves. A couple of Andamanese, who possibly chose to join mainstream society, came to meet the man. They were his assistants. The boys were introduced and it was comforting that they all spoke the same language. The man barked some instructions on their task stating that the two would help out the team. Finally, they all moved to the shore where a small boat was berthed. Not very dissimilar to the ones the boys had used for their travels.

They were thus able to help in getting the vessel to shore. The five of them sat and away it went to the Strait Island. On the way they discussed the plan of action. It was to meet a Great Andamanese family and discuss with them about how the government support had helped them. The island was visible from this shore and hence it did not take much time to hit the other shores. They chose a pre-determined spot with an anchor rope and tied the vessel to it. The few bags they had were then carried as they made their way inland. The island was not remarkably different from Baratang in terms of the initial settlements that they saw. But soon this gave way to dense vegetation. The boys and the man were comfortable traversing it but it was evident that the two assistants faced difficulty. They moved slowly as if danger lurked at every point. They were also uncomfortable with some insects and spiders on the leaves which had to be brushed aside to move forward. Soon they reached an opening and lo behold there was a settlement of the tribes. There was a man waiting for them in one of the huts and he came forward to greet the man. They spoke in a new language, which they later came to know was Koine. But he was fluent in Hindi too and what he spoke was a mixture of the two.

All five of them were taken to a hut where the family lived. The boys could see that the hut was not very different from where the man lived. After all the denizens of the forests would have used similar materials to build it. There was a couple and their one child in the hut. The man called them out and spoke to them. The conversations had to be translated and it seemed that the family was staying in the forests away from the other tribesmen for whom the government had built settlements. It seemed that they wanted to stay in their pristine surroundings and way of life rather than be dependent on doles. It suddenly dawned on the two that they had not visited the Great Andamanese settlement where the government had provided facilities but to a family choosing to live on its own terms in line with what their ancestors did. So this was the surprise that the man was referring to.

A lot of information came out in this rendezvous. They had agreed to the man talking to them since a level of confidence had built up and they were sure that he would not interfere with their way of life. Looked like this group wanted to maintain an isolationist policy. However, in the discussions it became clear that their son often went to the Tribal Settlement in the urge to eat the food that was served there. Rice, dal, vegetables cooked in heavy spices and even sweet dishes. Moreover, he was showing little interest in hunting, fishing or even gathering fruits and vegetables. The couple were not happy at this and wanted to move deeper into the forests to prevent his rendezvous. When they served the tradition meals, the expression of the boy was obvious.

The family talked about their life and even asked the two about theirs. While all this had to be translated by the man, it was obvious that the way of life was not very different. The family had lost a lot of its members to diseases and hence chose the way of life deep in the forest of Strait Island. They talked about their music and dance, some of which the family had managed to preserve. The boys also talked about their journey and the couple could not believe what they were hearing. The two were almost the age of their son and they had traversed the large seas. They were inquisitive about the mission of the boys and wished them luck. Of course, all this was capped by the five agreeing to go on a hunting expedition with the man. They were in luck as they managed to catch a boar. The two assistants were a bit taken aback by the cruelty of the kill but the boys found it quite similar to their earlier encounters with the other tribes. They carried the animal back and the woman and her son were overjoyed to see it. They prepared a big feast that night as all eight of them enjoyed the meat.

They all slept in the open on bamboo mats. Not a pleasant experience for the two assistants but they came to expect this on such study trips. As dawn hit, it was time to bid farewell. The man exchanged some gifts with the family. The Great Andamanese family also gave some trinkets made of bamboo to the boys. The parting was sombre and they left the family and moved towards the shore. When they reached the sea, another family of the tribe, this time from the settlements of the government was standing alongside the vessel looking at it. The man conversed with this group too. This time it was Hindi and all of them understood it. They all were fully clothed and looked to have blended well with the mainstream population. One of them wanted to go to Baratang. The man agreed and all six of them came on the vessel. On the way the tribesman told them that the government had given them all facilities and they were living a very different life from their forest cousins whom the five had visited. In a way it was a reflection of how things had changed? Whether for good or for bad?

****

CHAPTER XXIII

Trip down south

The interaction with this one Great Andamanese family that chose the sustainable way of life gave the boys so much perspective. The history was a chronology of how civilisation as we know it as altered the way of life for the indigenous people. They carried mixed feelings as they made their way back from the Strait Island and from Baratang onto the mainland of islands. Thoughts were now on probably the most precarious part of the journey, something about life and death. Could the boys make it?

The first challenge was to cross the Jarawa forests and move south. There was the risk of the authorities on their tail, if they chose the route of moving through the forests. It would also cause trouble for the Jarawas. However, they had the option of using a vehicle to cross the road. But then how would they catch hold of someone to take them across the reserve forests. Fortunately, there were some vehicles crossing the forests into the urban agglomerations of the island. The anthropologist helped them out with one such vehicle. There was a need for identification papers but these were managed as the two went through the forests. There were some Jarawas on the roadside. One of the vehicles ahead of them stopped and gave some biscuits to the children of the tribe. This was not allowed by the government but then some overzealous tourists resorted to this and wanted to take back memories of their interactions. The boys recollected what the Great Andamanese couple had told them on Strait Island. Their boy was being wooed by the interaction with the outside world and they were worried that he would not preserve their culture. Some of the boys looked at the two. To their shock, it was one of the Jarawa boys that the two had met. He came towards the vehicle and waved. Some of the other tourists in the vehicles were surprised at this gesture. The two waved back and for the first time one could smiles on the faces of the tribal children. The boys took care not to disembark as they told the driver to move ahead. He too was taken aback at this and enquired whether the boys knew the tribe. They gave a negated expression and the driver did not stop the vehicle and went along with the convoy. During the rest of the drive, there were other Jarawas as they peered at the convoy of vehicles driving. The boys also saw some workers along the road who were engaged in construction. A lot of dust was kicked as the convoy rolled through the terrain often on half baked roads.

Once the forest was over, the driver as instructed dropped the boys off at a location. From here they hitchhiked to a place called Wandoor which was connected by road. The boys had studied the geography and understood that they first needed to get to the Tarmugli island, a picturesque island well known for its crystal clear waters and coral reefs. It was the closest point to get to the North Sentinel Island. But that part of the journey was not going to be easy as no one was allowed there. There were navy boats patrolling the waters since there was an incident of a man, a missionary and preacher who was dropped off the island by fishermen. He was believed to have been killed by the tribesmen. So it was arguably the toughest challenge for the boys.

****

CHAPTER XXIV

Tarmugli and its beauty

The boys rested in Wandoor and decided to go to the Tarmugli island the next day. They enquired and found that a ferry went there the next day. They had some money with them and used it to buy two tickets. They passed off as Andamanese and no one suspected them. The journey was not very long as they reached the eastern shore of the island.

It was obvious that the waters were much clearer than the earlier islands that they had seen. There were hues of green and blue which gave an impression of a canvas splayed with colours. There were a lot of tourists on the ferry. They were surprised to see the two boys and enquired of them. Some of them had not seen a Shompen. The boys explained that they were from the Nicobarese tribe and had integrated with mainstream society. It was a surprise to the tourists who asked the boys many questions about the tribe. Both of them had seen the world around them and managed to evade any suspicions that may have been harboured by the questioners. It was obvious to the boys as to how little these people knew about the culture of the islands. After all they had come only for seeing the touristic spots, especially the beautiful beaches and marine life.

The trip was short as the ferries were much faster. It was for the first time that the boys were inside such a large vessel. They had only seen it from a distance in the waters. It had a large cabin with good seating capacity. They were selling eatables inside and some parents were purchasing it for their children. The vessel had an entire crew with a person in a white cap steering it and others helping out with tasks. The boys were overawed at the different lives they all lived in the forests. For them there were two different worlds in the same span of islands and both of them understood so little of each other. Some like the anthropologist whom they met on Strait Island were trying to bridge this seemingly vast schism.

They soon reached the shores of this new island. The landscape was prettier and the beaches were of white sand. However, the place where they berthed was crowded. The same feeling that the Shompen boy got when they went to the towns of the island chain. There was a flurry of activity with a market at the place too. Tourists were going around the shops and tourist operators were busy selling their packages. The boys managed to blend themselves in this chaos. Now they had to plan out on getting to the western end of the island. They did not want to think far about the most precarious part of the journey to the next island of the list. With their journey having been quite smooth as compared to expectations, they were optimistic.

They chose to move through the interior forests rather than risk being caught on the shores. Moreover, the woods were part of their life and they could traverse it. More importantly, it would prepare them for the next journey in the North Sentinel especially if they had to hide and avoid nasty encounters. After all that would surely be a matter of life and death. It was thick and there were no pathways to guide them. They had to move the shrubbery with their bare hands and a stick to move forward. They were also unsure about the ground and the dangers that it held. Snakes for one and then some insects which could have nasty bites. Although this was child's play, they were for an unknown reason more cautious. It was a new island and they wanted to replicate the fear that they would have in their next encounter. After some time as the sun was on top, they reached a pathway. This was surely going to take them to other end of the shore or so they had a hunch. It proved to be true as they soon hit the shores. It was a clean and pretty beach with all the markings of not being inhabited. There was something to this island that was so different from the others they had seen. The waters that spanned to the other end seemed blue with a touch of turquoise. It seemed inviting as if the Sentinelese were welcoming them across the waters. But here was the difficult part. They had no vessel and they had to look out for one.

So the boys rested on the sandy floor. Surveying the sea ahead of them and looking at the blue skies above. It was not going to be easy to cross this large mass of water in front of them. Then there was the danger of patrolling by the coast guard and navy. It was after all a protected area and they did not want even the fishermen to be near that place. There were weighing the options in front of them. Catch hold of some fishermen to get them across but then who would take the risk and even if they did, a hefty amount would be sought. Or else build a raft of local materials. But neither were the boys experts in building nor was there any guarantee that it would withstand the strong waves. And there was a good expanse of water between the two islands, actually around thirty five kilometres. No sooner that the boys were immersed in all these thoughts that a man walked out of the woods into the shore. He was clearly of negroid origin and was surprised to see the two boys.

In the conversation, it came to light that he was from the Onges tribe and had come to this island as a youngster. His parents had got him here and they were working in the farms. However, after they passed away, he chose to live on his own terms in the forests. No family, just living in isolation in woods which were not as dense as back in some of the islands of the archipelago. The man told them about his lifestyle of hunting and gathering food. Occasionally, he went fishing too. It was the turn of the boys to now reveal their story. Not very difficult for them to recount but the man was listening intently. It was as if he seemed to relate to them. He was particularly interested in the story of the Shompens and the Jangils. It was clear that he had not encountered any of them and had a keen interest to understand these tribes. Then he said, "*When I was you age, I wanted to do the same thing. Understand the indigenous people of our islands. When we came over to Tarmugli, I heard about the Sentinelese and the fact that this was the closest island to that prohibited paradise. And I did make two trips there. We call the forbidden island as Chankute. It has been my desire to understand the people inhabiting it.*"

Now it was the boys turn to gape in awe. "*The first one was unexpectedly good. I got some coconuts on my raft and gave it to some men who were on the shore. They were not aggressive and we even examined each other from close quarters. However, when someone called out to them, they made gestures to me to leave. Probably out of the fear that whoever called could harm me. So I left. In the distance, I saw a group of men with spears. They however did not show any aggression and merely watched me sail off. Then they seemed to be talking to the men on the beach, probably scolding them for having accepted the coconuts from a stranger.*" The boys had a lot of questions. "*How did they look? What did they say and could you understand them? What were they wearing? etc etc*". The man took a pause and responded.

"*They were slightly taller than us and even the Jarawas. However, their complexions were nearly the same. They wore a small belt and were covered with only leaves. However, in my next visit, it was risky and almost fatal. There was one boy and a girl who were on the shore when I landed. When I offered them coconuts, they accepted and smiled back. However, when they came close to me, a group of men, maybe around three or four, with spears attacked me. They threw some spears and one of it grazed my elbow. I fell but managed to gather myself and run towards the canoe. By the time the men reached the water, I was able to push my canoe to deeper waters. But they did not stop there. They threw their spears and one of it hit the canoe but did not topple it. I rowed with all my strength. But just as I thought I had reached a safe distance, I saw two of them on another canoe giving chase. These looked to be fishermen but now their intent was to catch me. I don't remember how I managed to row straining every sinew. I did not look back until I saw another vessel, this time of the navy. When I looked back, I could see the men in the canoe still behind me but their vessel was probably a bit more primitive and could not close the gap. When they saw the large vessel, they decided to give up and turned back. My ordeal was however not over as the navy vessel came close to me and checked me. They seemed hesitant to come closer and kept their distance. The skipper of the vessel sized me up and probably had a hunch that I was from the Sentinelese tribe. I realised this and did not want to speak up. I had not worn clothes so that I could gel with the indigenous people of the island. Then someone spoke to me in Hindi and I just acted as if I didn't understand. I also showed a lot of fear in my eyes. The men made a gesture to me to go back to the island. They did not even suspect seeing the boat which was better than what the Sentinelese had. They just motioned for me to move back to the island and left. I went to some distance and then started fishing."*

The boys heard all this was amazement. This was a first hand account that they heard from someone of this elusive tribe about which so little was known. The boys had studied about the shipwrecks which occurred on the island and how some people were killed. But hearing this from the horse's mouth was something else. It did fill a sense of trepidation since the second encounter of the man was precarious and could have cost him his life. If that canoe had toppled with that spear, he would have been fodder for the Sentinelese. It was all a matter of luck.

But the boys could not believe their stroke of fortune too. This was probably the best person they could have met on this island. Someone who had met the Sentinelese and one with nearly the same interest as them in meeting the indigenous people. It was also possible that he may be one of the few persons who could actually help out the boys to reach the prohibited island. The man it seemed could read their thoughts. He said, "*Let us first build a sturdy canoe and then all three of us will go to that island. I also need to make a trip and with you boys, I have the courage to do it despite the last encounter. We have to be careful though to keep out of the sight of the authorities and then pray that the tribesmen are more hospitable this time around. In my heart of hearts, I still believe that they are not aggressive. Perhaps they thought that I was going to harm the kids in the last encounter and hence chased me away."*

So the plan was made. The three began to work on the canoe. It was painstaking as they had to collect the wood, cane and the bamboo. The wooden planks and the cane had to be joined and the bamboo was to be woven. The Onges man was an expert and they managed to complete in by the time dusk fell. The presence of the three helped. Despite Tabo not feeling well, he provided whatever support he could. The ailment seemed to be affecting him more too often. Possibly due to the strain of the journey. He was not sure if he had the energy to complete the last leg of their tryst.

Once the structure of the canoe was made, they went back to his hut. It was deep in the woods and well hidden by the shrubbery around. The man had the same hut which the boys had seen in the Little Andamans. Made of tree trunks and canes, there was a bamboo sticks on which a platform was built. It was spacious and the boys suspected that apart from the man, others may also have visited the place. But the entire structure was covered with the thick growth of the trees and it was well masked. Unless, one came close and moved the undergrowth, the dwelling was well masked. The man welcomed them to the house. They prepared a meal outside by boiling the vegetables and rice. The man had grown the vegetables and he had a stock of rice. As dusk came, they had the meal and went off to sleep.

The tiredness of the day provided them a sound sleep. When the boys woke up, they found that the man was not there. Curious, they went out and found that the man was preparing his bags for the journey ahead. He saw them and said, "*Wash yourselves in the stream nearby and then we can have something to eat. Prepare yourself fast since we need to leave as early as we can.*" The boys quickly freshened themselves and were ready. They helped out in packing their provisions. The man also packed some knives which he had got from the market. It would be useful but no match for the Sentinelese spears if they were forced to self defend. After the light snacks of fruits, they were all prepared as they moved towards the shore where the canoe was berthed. When the boys saw the canoe, there was a hint of suspicion if this was sturdy enough. The man read their minds and said, "*This is very good vessel and will take us to the destination. We have enough space to store out stuff too. Let us move.*"

****

CHAPTER XXV

Journey to the unknown

So the canoe was pushed into the deep waters. They all got aboard and started rowing. There were some other fishing vessels but they were busy with their catch. Some of them looked at the large canoe but did not probe much. The three rowed into the deep waters with their oars. The boys were surprised at how sturdy and fast the vessel was. This was much better than the canoes that they had travelled or seen. The Onges were known to be experts in deep sea fishing and this man had prepared one such vessel.

The boys could see shoals of fish but this was not the time to admire. The island they came from had disappeared from sight. Even the fishing vessels seemed to be limited as they moved deeper into the sea. One of the vessels which was close to them tried to shout out. But they could hear nothing. The man said, "*They are probably trying to warn us not to go towards the island. There would be the navy vessels patrolling. And then fishermen were not supposed to be going in the direction of the island. Let us hope they do not notify the authorities of us.*" There was danger at every step of this journey.

They slowly went deeper into the waters and the boys could see that the pace was quite good. The vessel was making substantial ground They were rowing in turns with two of them doing it at a time. Tibo was not very well due to the recurrence of his ailment but he too contributed in the effort. After a good couple of hours of rowing, they all rested. The bags were opened and they had some food. Fresh water was also carried and they all sipped it from the conical bamboo leaves in which it was stored. They splashed some sea water on their faces to cool down. The sun was beating down upon the canoe and they had to cover their heads for some shade. After a small nap, they all got up for the next leg. There were no boats or vessels in the horizon and they seemed all alone on the seas.

They set a good pace but with the choppy waters and no land horizon, it was difficult to gauge the progress being made. Shoals of fish were following the canoe. Then in the distance, they saw a vessel. It was in a perpendicular direction of their path. The two boys were rowing at a frenetic pace. The Onges man kept surveying this vessel. When it was coming closer, he signalled that this was a navy boat and they needed to go faster. He took over the rowing from Tibo as the boy was still not fully fit. They moved forward in the direction of North Sentinel. Tibo provided the commentary on the vessel closing in on them. The man said, "*These are motorised vessels and we stand no chance of outpacing them. Our only hope is that they mistake it for a canoe of the Sentinelese. But I am not sure the tribesmen come this far for fishing.*"

No sooner had he said this that the Shompen boy shouted. "*I see some land ahead. Look at those treelines.*" The others could barely make out anything but he was confident. "*My eyesight is good and I can surely tell that this is the island we came for. We can easily reach the place before the navy boat catches us. Let us put all the effort now. If we are caught, then all our journey would be of no use.*" With this they rowed faster. With time the silhouette of the island became clearer and the other two were also ecstatic. It was indeed the island and they had reached pretty fast. Even the Onges man seemed to be surprised at the pace they had set and how fast they had reached their destination. "*This is amazing. We have reached the place in a few hours. It took me almost a day the last time I did this journey. But the vessel is still behind us and we need to move faster. You guys duck and lie flat and I will row. When they see me, they could mistake me for a Sentinelese and avoid.*"

This is exactly what happened. As the boys lay flat on the canoe, the vessel chasing them seemed to slow down. It merely kept a watch at a distance and did not bridge the gap. The canoe thus moved closer to the island. However, once they were around a kilometre of the island, they stopped. This was the time to gather all the courage and see where they should berth the vessel. If they were spotted by the Sentinelese, it would all be over. They would then need to circle and decided on a suitable spot. From their distance, the Shompen boy thought that he sighted some people. "*I think it was some of the tribesmen in that clearing. They were looking in the general direction of the sea and not specifically at us. So it is better we avoid that place. Let us go around the island and look for a better spot.*" With their experience of the sighting of the island itself, the other two had to go by what Kayat had thought he saw. They agreed to look for another spot and went around the island. After travelling a distance, they saw a clearing and decided to try that spot. Finally, they moved closer to scan the place. The coast seemed clear and it looked like an apt location.

At a snail's pace they moved closer. The hearts were beating faster. Despite the Onges experience, he too had palpitations especially after his last encounter. The boys despite their long journey were coming to the last phase of probably their most dangerous tryst. They were scared. The kept scouting the horizon but didn't see anyone. But yet many negative thoughts ran through their mind. Some visualisation of the tribesmen coming with spears all ready to kill them. Many had indicated that these tribesmen were also inclined towards cannibalism and this scared them.

But then with a final show of bravado, they moved closer to the beach. The waters became shallow. It was crystal clear and the beach was sparklingly white with the clean sands. But this was no time to admire the beauty of this island. It was a matter of life and death. With trepidation and tip toed steps, they moved closer to the island. The boat was ashore. There was no going back. The skin of all three turned red as in a way they feared an imminent attack. All they had were knives in their bagpack and this was scant comfort. They lost the focus on the boat and were more concerned about someone in the bushes. They dragged the canoe and berthed it in the thick shrubbery. As soon as they turned to go back to the shores, someone came out to the clearing not far from them. They all froze.

****

CHAPTER XXVI

Encounter with the Sentinelese

It was a young woman who came out of the bushes. She had apparently not seen them and they used this opportunity to hide. There was some noise and she looked towards the bushes but could not catch hold of them. She could also not make out the canoe despite some parts of its jutting out through the greenery. She waited and watched as if she suspected someone. Then she called out in a strange tone. Out came a young man with a spear. At the sight of the weapon, the fear level of the three rose. Apparently they were well built and had only a bark belt and some leaves on them. They spoke something and the girl pointed in the direction of where the three were hiding. The boy then asked her to wait and came in the direction.

There was no option but for the three to move in deeper into the forests. It was much denser than the forests that they had seen in their islands. In a way, it was untouched by civilisation and had preserved its beauty. Out of fear they ran but had to stop to catch a breadth. There were amidst a dense cover and no one seemed to be following them. The Onges man was the first to break the silence. "*Don't think the man is coming after us. But we are now in the forbidden island. Let us see what fate has in store for us.*"

Tibo was feeling a bit unwell and weak. The journey and this escape from the two Sentinelese had exacerbated it. They decided to take a break and eat some fruits which they had. The rest was well deserved as the pace set for the escape was frenetic. Now the plan was to return to the same place where their canoe was berthed. Going deeper into the woods would carry the risk of being caught by the community. But finding the way back was not going to be easy. The Onges man was however confident and since all of them were literally the children of the forests, they managed to have the general direction. The traces of their escape helped to retrace the path.

They trudged for some time at a slow pace. The Nicobarese boy was still unwell but his spirits were high. They had all reached the final island of their tryst and were still alive. Probably no one apart from the colonial powers had stayed in the island for so long. At a distance, they could now hear the splashing of the waters. It was clear but there were still woods in front of them. They could not be far from the sea as also the place where their canoe was berthed. No sooner were they out of the bushes that a spear came flying in their way. It just whizzed past the three but at a good distance. Whoever threw it either was a novice or missed intentionally just to scare them. Then there was panic all around and they all ran helter and skelter. In the confusion, Tibo fell down more from exhaustion than anything else. The other two looked back at their companion but could do nothing.

As the Nicobarese boy looked up, he saw two set of eyes gazing at him. But there was no anger, just curiosity. He let out a scream as the other two stopped. They were the young boy and the girl. The latter gave her hand but the boy was too petrified to reciprocate. He was too exhausted and just collapsed. He did not know how time passed but after sometime came to his senses. The two were pouring splashing some seawater for him to come out of his stupor. The were examining his eyes and nose. Tibo was shocked. He did not know how to respond. His body was too weak and there was no use in attempting to escape. Surely the two who had thrown a spear would now kill him. They were talking in a strange language which be presumed would be Sentinelese. He was just waiting for the moment when they would put him out of his misery. The memories of his parents and friends came to light. Thoughts about why he undertook this journey with his medical condition? What was the purpose of life? He believed that no one would find his body.

That decisive moment didn't come for a long time. He was surprised as the two were still sizing him up and talking. However, what shocked him was that their expression and the tone which did not suggest anger or hatred. They were calmly examining him like a new specie. Feeling his forehead, chest, arms, and legs. They did not undress him though. With the passage of time, the boy became calmer and the negative thoughts slowly disappeared. He was running a temperature and the two seemed concerned on that as they felt his forehead time and again. They spoke something to him but the boy did not know how to respond. He just said that he was fine and they seemed to understand the intent. They both smiled and gave him some water to drink. Tibo has no option. He could just pray that the two did not harm him or take him to the community, wherein the reaction would be uncertain..

Both the Onges man and the Shompen boy had a greater level of shock. They retraced their steps back and saw the two Sentinelese youngsters examine their friend. While Kayat wanted to confront them, the man held him back. "*Don't show your bravado. If they wanted to kill him, they would have. They seem to be curious about something. Looks like that they are trying to treat him.*" He was correct. Slowly the two carried the boy, one holding both legs and the other both arms into the woods. They followed from a distance. The Onges man was sure that the two knew that they were being followed but did not want to alarm them. Their focus was after all on the boy. They took the boy to a lone shelter which seemed abandoned. Gauging by the poor condition of its slanting roof and entrance where there was a lot of growth of plants.

It was built out of similar materials that was used back in the islands. After all similar climatic conditions and flora would lead to quite similar responses. Once the two entered the shelter, Kayat and the man could not see what was happening. After sometime, the girl came out and went in a particular direction. The two were tempted to go into the hut and confront the Sentinelese boy but they chose to keep a distance. The girl came back to the hut this time with a woman and they were carrying something. The woman seemed elderly and the two looked around for anyone. They could not spot the two who were hiding in the bushes. They went in and came out much later. The woman quietly tiptoed away after checking if the coast was clear. It looked obvious that whatever was happening in the hut was in top secrecy. Probably they did not want the others to know about it.

Tibo himself was stunned by the turn of events. He was counting the last seconds of his life and here he was lying in a hut. Both the youngsters had tended to him like his siblings despite knowing fully well that he was an outsider. They rubbed a paste on his forehead and chest. And then they had called the woman who gave the boy something to eat. He was initially hesitant but they literally made him swallow it by opening his mouth. It tasted pretty awful, but they just about managed to make him eat it. It was comical and when the boy finally managed to swallow a good portion they let out a smile. Tibo was not sure how to react but he went along with whatever he was being subject to. The hut had a mat which was comfortable. As the day progressed, he felt better and the temperature seemed to come down. He was surprised at the efficacy of whatever was given to him.

As the sun was setting, the girl went back and got something to eat. It was some fruits and berries. She took some inside and kept some on the porch of the house. It was now obvious that the two Sentinelese were certain that the dwelling was being watched by the two people who had come to this island. As she kept the fruits outside, she made a gesture in a general direction for the two to come and eat it. Then she quietly slipped away with the boy. The youngsters were indeed smart as they cared for the three visitors on their island. But the three wondered as to the motive behind all this. They were all under the impression that the tribe was aggressive and would not spare them. But here the two were taking a risk by tending to three outsiders. However, they were doing this in secrecy and this probably displayed the fact that the reaction of the rest of the tribesmen would be uncertain to all this. Maybe the community elders would oppose all this and even kill these trespassers.

As soon as the two left, the Onges man and Kayat did not want to take a risk and go to the hut. There was a chance that the youngsters may come back. They waited till it was dusk and the road was clear. They then went to the hut. They saw the structure clearly for the first time. It was made of cane fibre but the roof was sloping and touched the ground at the other end. On the sides, natural growth of leaves was used to cover from three sides. It was open on one side. Quite unlike the huts back in the forests. A bit more primitive but this may not have been the huts where the community was staying. They saw Tibo and the Shompen boy burst out in tears. The Onges man also touched the boy and asked, "*What have they put on your forehead. It looks like a leaf.*"

The Nicobarese boy was stumped for a while. He first looked at the two unable to comprehend the environment around. Whatever was given to him had a sedative effect. But as his eyes adjusted, he could make out the two and only smiled. The only words that came out of him was "*I am fine.*" He then went back to a state of stupor. The two understood that the boy needed some rest. But they too were surprised at the response of the two youngsters. Strangers who were tending to this boy despite all the risks. Maybe his condition evoked a sense a sympathy. And who was this woman who came. Maybe someone who had some knowledge of treatment just like the medicine man back home. It all looked so perplexing to the two since they had heard horror stories of the tribe.

Finally, they offered some of the fruits left behind to Tibo but he had slept off. They too went out and surveyed the place to check if anyone was around. There was an eerie feeling that the youngsters were keeping watch on them from a distance just like they had done. But the growth was too dense to spot anyone. However, even if they were, the two could do nothing with their friend ill and the island full of the tribesmen which had deadly weapons like arrows and spears. They went back to the shelter and lay on the side of their friend. Sleep came early with all the vigour of their activities during the day.

No sooner did they wake up that three sets of eyes were staring down upon them. The youngsters and another man. Before they could react, the two were pinned down on their shoulders with enough power that they were unable to respond. All of them seemed powerful. It was best not to react and the two just lay still. Now the gaze was completely on the Onges man. Not surprising since he was the only one of Negrito features among the three. They said something to him and he responded in Onge but they could not understand. They were still fixated on him and probably their thoughts were along the line of "*Who is this outsider who looks very much like us.*"

Once the two did not react to the pinning down, the man asked them again in Sentinelese but they could not understand. Since they were pinned down, they could not make any gestures too. Finally, they released their shoulders and the two sat up. They were frightened but yet there was a feeling of calmness in that there was nothing to lose and they were still alive. Moreover, apart from that missed spear, which albeit may have been intentional, there was nothing to indicate that the tribesmen they encountered were aggressive. The youngster and the man also sat down on the floor. They were naked except for a belt made of some natural fibre. For the Onges man and the Shompen boy, this was not surprising as they too were children of the forest. There was some exchange of language but neither could follow each other. The Shompen boy could pick up some cues in the expressions but he too found it tough without any foundation. It was a language on which there was no information available anywhere. Not surprising since there was little interaction of the outside world with this civilisation.

With the talk yielding little progress, the only option left was gestures. The Sentinelese man pointed to Tibo and gave an expression suggesting that he was ill. He then gestured indicating that they were trying to cure him. The Shompen boy picked up these cues and told the Onges man who was still perplexed at the gestures. The tribesmen understood that the boy was a good translator and the man again specifically gestured something to Kayat. The boy translated these gestures into something along the lines that "*Don't worry. We will not kill you. But you better stay here. It is not safe to go outside.*" He responded with his own gestures wanting to say that, "*We came to meet you all as friends and study your culture. We do not want to harm any of you.*" However, he was not sure whether they could understand it. By the look on their expressions, it seemed that the girl probably understood something as she told the others. They all smiled back.

But this gesticulated conversation had lightened the mood and the fear of each other subsided. The Onges man then asked Kayat to tell them that they had bought some gifts for the tribesmen. Kayat tried his best to act it out but the three were surprised. This time it was the boy who probably understood it as he gestured to the two to go and get it. They left the girl in the hut while all four went towards the shore. After walking briskly through the woods led by the Sentinelese boy, they reached the shore. Then the two visitors searched around and found the place where their boat was hidden. Both the tribesmen surveyed the vessel with intent. They were overawed by its size and structure as they gesticulated that it was large. The Onges man and the Shompen boy then took out the coconuts they had brought with them. The tribesmen were so happy to see the fruit. An earlier expedition of anthropologists had also given coconuts to the tribe. The Shompen boy then took out a tool and cut it showing the tribesmen how to drink the water inside. He then took out the shell and had a part of the white skin inside. The tribesman followed him and their expression indicated that both the water and the white mass were tasty. The youngster followed suit and he too enjoyed it. They washed themselves in the sea and then carried the bag of coconuts back to the shelter.

As they moved through the forest, the man motioned for them to stop. There was a sound in the distance as the four kept silent. A group of some Sentinelese with some hunting tools passed by. They had some bows and arrows as well as spears. They seemed to be headed to the shore but in a slightly different direction. It was strange that the two shielded the visitors from them. Once the group was out of earshot, the youngster gestured. The Shompen boy could make out that they considered that the men may not like to see the two and could even harm them. The visitors believed all this and they had no option since they were at the mercy of the three. Meanwhile the girl was tending to Tibo. She changed the cloth on his forehead and gave him something to eat. It was a private moment for the two as it increased their bonding. She made him sit up and gave him some water to drink. Tibo was still groggy from the effect of what was given to him but he was feeling better. His temperature was also under control though he still felt quite weak. She held his hand softly to give him some comfort. It was something which he never expected from a Sentinelese girl. It was almost like a dream.

When the others came in, the girl was still holding his hand. Kayat was a bit taken aback at this. They had just met the evening before and it was almost like a family member caring for the boy. He had never expected to see the softer side of the tribe after hearing so much. The girl gestured that the Nicobarese boy looked better and would be fine very soon. Kayat conveyed this message but Tibo spoke for himself. "*I can understand what she is trying to say.*" His friend responded, "*No doubt, I am sure both of you know each other so well.*" And he laughed. The Onges man too joined in the humour. And to their surprise the two Sentinelese also seemed to have got the message and they too smiled.

The girl blushed. Tibo too was in an awkward situation but he kept mum. She removed her hand and moved away towards the other two tribesmen. They gave her one of the coconuts which she surveyed. She was told the technique to drink the water and eat the white matter within. She too enjoyed the taste which brought a smile to her face.

The six of them were now in the shelter and trying to converse. Kayat was able to understand many of the gestures and even picked up a few words of the language spoken by the three. The conversation centred around the Sentinelese and their life. How many years ago some of the outsiders had come and spread disease among them. Some of even came with arms and killed them or took them to other places. The reason why people hate them and don't want to intermingle. Stories of why some people who came were killed. The Shompen boy also tried to convey the message of how they had come to the island after traversing long distances across the island chain. The tribesmen could pick up only a few nuances but they were indeed surprised. All this effort despite one of the boys afflicted with a strange condition.

The tales went on only to be interrupted for the afternoon lunch. The sun was up and beating down on the shelter. The shade was a blessing though. They ate some coconuts first and then the four went in search of some fruits. The girl stayed back to nurse Tibo. They found some pandunus and plucked it. As soon as they had enough stock, they decided to retrace the steps. While returning, they heard some noise and stopped. This time there was no encounter since the group was at a distance from them. However, what was clear was that the area was habited or atleast used as a journey pathway by the others of the tribe. Hence, they had to be watchful at every step.

The six then sat together and had a hearty meal. The three visitors never thought of such a reception from the islanders who were considered hostile by the rest of the world. The little information they gathered through gestures gave an impression that the animosity stemmed from the history of contacts. Each such contact had left an indelible scarred imprint either due to some members being taken away or afflicted with disease or even harassed. Thus over the years, the attitude had been of caution and dissuasion. Sometimes when the point of inflexion was passed, it gave way to aggression and violence. With this form of communication, it was clear that language was no longer a barrier. The six had formed a bond even in this limited interaction.

This went on for a few days as Tibo was being nursed by the tribesmen. Occasionally, the woman would also come. She seemed to be the physician for the tribe and dealt with the collection and concoction of the medicinal plants. She would make a thorough check of the Nicobarese boy. Probably he was like a guinea pig for testing out the efficacy of her medicine. Whatever, it was, the boy felt much better. Even the hospitals of the towns could not cure his ailment and here were the medicines of an uncontacted civilisation which seemed to be bearing fruition. Made one wonder on the very foundation of civilisational evolution.

As time passed, the boy recovered well and stopped having the irregular bouts of fever. He also felt rejuvenated and the tiredness slowly dissipated. As the days wore on, all three of them felt the island being their home. They had literally forgotten their origins and home. The Shompen boy had picked up some words and was in a position to even communicate. There were some gaffes and laughs but then he knew no fear and tried to communicate with his accent. The Onges man found some of the words similar to his language which was a surprise. But the key aspect was that they were not caught. They managed to evade any patrols who probably avoided the shelter. The shelter itself was an old one which had been abandoned by the community. However, now it had been spruced up as the three were staying.

Life for the three was not very dissimilar to what they experienced in the woods of their islands. The only difference was that they did not go into the sea for fishing since it was risky. However, the did see some of the tribes taking their boats out in the water. But these vessels were quite primitive and did not venture out into the deep sea. But the nets and spears were very similar. The fishermen of the island had no contact with the outside world and hence little exposure to new equipment or vessels which would have aided them in improving the catch. But so was their general way of life. Be in the houses they made or the little cultivation they carried out. All of this was shown by the three to the Onges man and the Shompen boy in some of their travels. But they had to be careful in these adventures since the community was quite large and were roaming around the forests in search of food and hunting for animals. The three were recreating their own life in the woods though Tibo largely preferred to stay put as he was under treatment.

But for the Nicobarese boy, there was a whole new dimension to life. He was getting better in terms of his health, something which had troubled him for a long time since birth. On the other hand, the Sentinelese girl was now getting close to him. They were both developing feelings for each other. The proximity and the treatment may have stirred it. Despite the language barrier, it was evident to both the Onges man and Kayat that the two had developed a bond. So one day Kayat blurted out his thoughts to his friend, "*Are you serious about this girl. She is from one of the tribes dreaded by everyone. First of all her own family may not accept it if they get to know. They may also get aggressive on this count. Secondly, where do you plan to stay of this happens.*" Tibo though for a moment and then responded, "*I don't what is in store for both of us. But we surely like each other. I don't know about her but I don't mind staying in this island. Going outside will only expose her to another world. And I owe her my life and health.*"

The Shompen boy had enough cues. He decided to communicate it to the girl. In a mixture of some words and gestures, the conversation began with all the six in the shelter. From what transpired and as interpreted by Kayat, she too was serious about the relationship. She did not mind leaving the island despite whatever negative feedback her ancestors had provided about the harassment by outsiders. She was reluctant to talk to her family now until the boy was completely cured. She said that her mother was aware of the relationship and did not have any objection. But the elders of the community including the father would surely object and could even turn aggressive. Hence, she was waiting for the right time when the boy recovered fully.

It was indeed a strange situation but something all the protagonists in this drama had not foreseen. Seeing the Sentinelese from close quarters was what the three travellers had aspired but here it was a whole new twist. A melodramatic plot. They were living in the forests just like the tribe and actually enjoying it. As someone said, "*An island is a refuge for the soul, a place to reconnect with nature and rediscover ourselves*". They were indeed rediscovering themselves. Of course, they missed fishing in the open waters but that was a risk they could not take. Now they had to solve two elements of the conundrum, getting the relationship of the two kicking and finding a way to amicably meet the other members of the tribe. This was not going to be easy. Moreover, they had a premonition of something ugly coming up.

****

CHAPTER XXVII

The Final Escape

As the three lived their new life on the island with the support from the four Sentinelese, it was too good to be true for long. And that is precisely what happened. One of the boys of the community who also had feelings for the girl, suspected that she went somewhere with the other two. So one day, he tailed them until the shelter.

And what happened after that was straight out of a movie scene. He informed the community elders and they confronted the parents of the girl. The father pleaded ignorance while the mother accepted that she knew. There was a lot of discussion especially on the fact that the boy was seriously ill and was being nursed back to health. Even the physician was asked about her role and she said that it was her duty to treat anyone.

Once the three Sentinelese got to know about this development, they immediately rushed back to the shelter and asked the others to vacate the place and move elsewhere. They had another spot in mind where there was one such dilapidated shelter. But it was not as safe as this one and was closer to the shore thereby facilitating access. So they all rushed to that spot. It was definitely not as big as the earlier one and needed a lot of cleaning up to make it liveable. So they all got to work on that to remove all the plants and clean up the place.

Then Tibo said something which was in his mind during their earlier stay. "*I have decided to stay in this island with this girl. No matter what the outcome. Even if they come after me and harm me, I do not want to leave this place. Both of you leave on your own since it may not be safe for you in these circumstances. The boat is there and you can make good your escape. If they kill me, so be it. That is my fate and I have made my decision.*" Profound words which the Shompen boy translated for the other three. It was an emotional moment as the girl looked towards Tibo with a loving expression. She had clearly understood the translation and she went over and hugged him. The Nicobarese boy also could not hold back his tears.

Then suddenly a noise was heard in the bushes. The men had come looking for the three in this new shelter. They had suspected that they would be taken here and this was vindicated. The girl took Tibo by her hand and ran in one direction. He just had time to wave goodbye to his two friends. The other two Sentinelese took the Onges man and the Shompen boy in the direction of the boat. It was now or never. If the two were caught, it would be curtains. The two ran with whatever energy they had and soon reached the shore where the boat was berthed. They quickly cleaned up the shrubbery around it and cleaned the dirt on it. Then all four of them dragged the boat towards the shore. As soon as the vessel hit the water, the two climbed aboard and started rowing. They even forgot to say goodbye to the people who had helped them in this ordeal. Probably that split second decision not to waste any more time was fortuitus since out came a group of around six or seven men with bows and arrows. But strangely there was no menacing expression. They did not even point their weapons at the two despite them being in range of the arrows. It was as if they were just chasing them away from their abode without any harm. They made some gestures but the boys were looking the other way and rowing off to the deep sea. They briefly looked back and were surprised to see all the men and the two saviours waving at them. It was like a farewell to the visitors. As they moved deeper into the waters, they took a break. All thoughts came to their mind, "*Why did the Sentinelese not attack them? What would happen to Tibo? If they spared him, would he marry the girl? etc etc*". But both of them felt one thing, the tribe was not what the outside world had portrayed.

As they moved ahead towards Tarmugli, they heard a hoot ahead. It was navy ship that was coming towards them. Both of them cared little about it. After all the journey of discovery of the island archipelago was over. And they were sure that Tibo was in safe hands in the forbidden island. The only thought that came to their mind was "*The islands were in safe hands of the indigenous people. They were after all the spiritual guardians of the archipelago.*"

****

www.ingramcontent.com/pod-product-compliance
Lightning Source LLC
LaVergne TN
LVHW091324150826
845673LV00006B/1765
9798896991663